Lost in Clover

By Travis Richardson

Lost in Clover

By Travis Richardson

ISBN-13:978-1611874662
ISBN-10:1611874661

http://www.untreedreads.com
http://tsrichardson.com

This book is dedicated to Jason Furnish of Paola, KS. 1974-2012.

PART 1

CLOVER

1. FOOTBALL

"Rogers. Jeremy. Wake up, son."

Jeremy had drifted into an ether of pastel colors and cotton candy clouds. It was nice until he heard that voice and felt the pain. His head throbbed. He was on his back, and it was hot, unbearably hot. Opening his eyes he could make out somebody. He squinted. Who was looking at him? Oh right, Coach Sumner.

"Now watch my finger. Follow it," the coach said, waving the finger back and forth.

"I'm fine, Coach," Jeremy said, trying to remove his helmet.

"Whoa, hold on there, Rogers. Cooper clocked you solid. You've been out for at least 30 seconds. Can you move your arms and legs?"

Jeremy lifted, bent, and rotated all four limbs until Coach Sumner nodded and pulled him up. The team, the Clover Cavaliers, stood in a semi-circle, gazing at him with concern in their eyes. All the Cavaliers except for Crazy Eddie Cooper. The fourteen-year-old freshman already stood over six foot and weighed 220 pounds. Even though he was young, he was destined to be varsity that year. He looked disappointed—as if it were a crying shame that Jeremy was still alive.

It had been a simple drill. Coach Sumner had held out his stopwatch and timed how quickly the defense could break through the offensive line. And vice-versa, how long the offensive line could hold—which was three seconds. Jeremy, a presumed non-starter like most freshmen, had held the football as a faux quarterback. He had been the target for the defense and hadn't been allowed to move. When a lineman penetrated the line, they were rewarded with an easy sack. The unspoken rule was that the tackle should be hard enough to show the coach you meant it, but not to injure the ball holder. When Crazy Eddie broke through, he had lowered his head and speared Jeremy, helmet to helmet.

Even as an assistant coach escorted Jeremy off the field to take him to the hospital in Emporia, Jeremy sensed Crazy Eddie's lingering disappointment. Jeremy and most of his classmates had long suspected Crazy Eddie wanted to kill somebody bad. He wore a constant hostile glare backed with cold eyes that were incapable of sympathy. It seemed he was held in check by the teachers and the meanest son-of-a-bitch dad in Southeast Kansas. Crazy Eddie would go on to injure more teammates, including the starting quarterback, and so many opponents that the Grover

Wildcats forfeited in fear. But he didn't kill anybody, at least not that year…it was the next.

2. ROOFING
A YEAR LATER

Jeremy sat on top of a roof, sweating bullets. How he hated Kansas summers. Ninety-five degrees plus humidity felt more like 115. He had spent the morning stripping off old shingles with a claw-toothed shovel—bending forward, shoving those jagged metal teeth under a nail, but not into the wood—that was a no-no—and then pulling up on the unanchored weathered shingle, he'd chuck it in the vicinity of a trash bin, only to start on the next one. There were hundreds of them.

A tornado had blown through in mid-May. It hadn't leveled anything other than a barn, but the accompanying high winds and marble-sized hail had damaged many roofs and cars. Insurance claims had been processed and dozens of Clover homes were approved to be reshingled. Jeremy had been content mowing neighborhood lawns, but when L.T. Diamond, a contractor and deacon of the Prairie View Methodist, told Jeremy's dad the wage he was paying, there was no escaping destiny.

Jeremy was finished with one side of the roof and was halfway done with the other when he saw the actual roofers arriving with new shingles, roofing felt, and nail guns in the back of a truck. To Jeremy it felt like his job, not unlike football practice, was to do the dirty work so the others got the glory. L.T.'s son, Kevin, backed into the driveway in his spanking new smoke-gray Chevy Silverado. The wheels were jacked up high and, though the tinted windows were up, Jeremy heard Toby Keith loud and clear.

Kevin jumped out, his wiry shoulders and arms angling out of his University of Kansas Jayhawks basketball jersey. He was twenty and acted as if he owned Clover, a view that few residents opposed. He sized up Jeremy's work. Randy, a red-faced, pint-sized buddy with a beer gut, ambled over from the passenger side. He looked at Kevin, then the house, and sneered. "That's all you've done, Rogers? My grandmother could've done more."

"And she's got an artificial hip," Kevin added.

"Two of 'em."

They laughed over a pinch of Skoal. Jeremy stood, an aching tightness radiating through his lower back. "The other side is totally done."

"Yeah, but you don't finish the job sitting on your ass. Randy, show him how it's done." Randy shot Kevin a wounded look. "Come on now," Kevin said with a shove. "Show him how you became Diamond Contractors' top roofer."

Randy scaled up the ladder and onto the roof with unexpected speed and nimbleness. He grabbed the shovel from Jeremy, almost knocking him off.

"Watch and learn, son."

Randy shoved the clawed shovel under a nail and removed the shingle in a second. He attacked the rest of the row.

"Go Randy, go!" Kevin shouted from below.

Randy sweated furiously as he ripped shingles off with a fluid precision that nobody would have expected from the short, round man. He finished the row with a yelp, and Kevin howled below. Randy handed the shovel to Jeremy.

"That's the way you do it, son."

"Let's see if you can match that, Rogers," Kevin shouted.

Jeremy's back and shoulders burned while Randy and Kevin shouted at him. He tried to keep Randy's match, but it wasn't possible. He tore into the wood more than once.

"Dang Rogers, don't poke a hole in their ceiling. That's a different job," Randy said.

Jeremy was dizzy by the time he unhinged the final shingle. He wanted to quit right there, but Randy and Kevin clapped and invited him down for some Gatorade in the shade. Jeremy sat under a tree catching his breath and wiping condensation from the bottle across his face.

"What do you think his chances of being a full time contractor are?" Kevin asked Randy.

Randy looked at Jeremy for a moment as if he were a complex mathematical equation. "I've seen worse."

"I'd say he did alright. Alright for sure. Look Jeremy, we're going to a barbeque tonight. You want to come along?"

Jeremy noticed the glance that Randy shot over to Kevin.

"Sure, why not," Jeremy said, trying to play it cool.

"Alright then, let's get these shingles up on the roof so we can have a good time tonight with a clear conscience."

3. THE BARBEQUE

The barbeque was in a trailer park, and not the good one either. The Hancock Arms had a reputation for dropouts, ex-cons, the unemployed, and other people who can't seem to scrape bad luck off their shoe. Jeremy had called his parents to let them know he'd be with Kevin that night, location unspecified. They approved. Kevin was a good Methodist kid Jeremy could look up to.

"Drink up," Kevin said, handing Jeremy a beer.

"But…"

"Don't worry about it. This place is like Vegas; nobody says nothing to nobody about what happens here. That includes you. Anything you see tonight, you didn't see, understood?"

Jeremy nodded and took a sip. He felt dangerous, holding a beer out in the open. It wasn't like sneaking a bottle down to Matt Hendershot's basement; this was wide-open public display of drinking. Energy surged through his body with each sour taste. They walked behind a couple of beaten trailers to a barbeque pit full of orange embers with a runty pig hanging on a spit. Jeremy knew most of the guys who were gathered around the pit. They were a who's who of recent Clover High grads who didn't leave town or get married. Jeremy thought they looked older than they should have. Potbellies stretching through faded, stained T-shirts and bloated unshaven faces with dark circled eyes seemed to be the uniform.

"Hi," Jeremy said to the group.

"Rogers, how the hell are ya?" said Trevor McDaniels, the previous year's starting quarterback until Crazy Eddie broke his arm. It took Jeremy half a second to recognize him, he had deteriorated that quickly. They shook hands, and Trevor put his arm around Jeremy. "This guy also got injured by Crazy Eddie. He was the first one that bastard clocked seriously. What happened again?"

"Concussion. Just a line drill, but he speared me—helmet to helmet."

A guy with a trucker hat asked, "Do you still play?"

Jeremy shook his head. "Doctor didn't think I'd be safe."

In truth the doctor didn't want anybody to participate in full contact football, but it was his mother who forbade him to play after that hit. Regardless, Jeremy hated Crazy Eddie for destroying his dream of high school football glory.

"Yeah, the guy is a freaking maniac. Somebody needs to stop him," Trevor said. "I should be in college taking snaps, dammit. Northeastern State and some Arkansas schools were interested in me. But not with a broken arm. I'm damaged goods."

"Come on now, Trevor," Kevin said with a smile. "You really think you would've got into college with your grades?"

A chuckle floated in the air. Trevor moved from foot to foot, his eyes burning. He threw his beer bottle over a mound in the distance.

"I could've. Besides, they help athletes in college on tests and stuff... And that asshole took that away from me. And he's only fifteen. I mean, who does he think he is?"

"We need to teach him something," said a bearded slacker that Jeremy had never met.

"Did you hear what he did to a fella up in Harrisburg?" Randy asked, pausing to spit out tobacco juice. "Seems this guy was dating one of Eddie's sisters. Ashley I think, don't know. They're all skanks. Anyhow, something goes wrong and the sister comes crying to her little brother. So Crazy Eddie takes a bat up to his house and beats the guy within an inch of his life. He's in a body cast and everything, but won't press charges because he doesn't want to admit a fifteen-year-old whipped his ass."

The guys laughed.

"He isn't a normal fifteen-year-old. He's a mongoloid," Kevin said.

"Somebody needs to put him in his place before he does any more damage," Trevor slurred. "He's only going to get bigger and meaner, you know. It's like a public safety issue."

"Let's kill Cooper!" Randy shouted.

"Kill Cooper! Kill Cooper!" Trevor chanted until everybody at the barbeque joined the anthem.

4. DIRECTIONS

After the scrawny pig was devoured and more beers knocked back, the rhetoric escalated. It seemed that Crazy Eddie had given everybody their lot in life. All personal failures were accounted for by a fifteen-year-old giant. Everybody had a grievance against Crazy Eddie whether they had met him or not, and now was the time to take care of the situation. Beer cans were crushed, and new ones opened. Voices grew louder and more impassioned.

Buzzed, Jeremy enjoyed the anger. Crazy Eddie had this coming. He had never apologized for the tackle, and he had refused eye contact for the rest of the school year. Jeremy felt he knew Crazy Eddie better than anybody else at the barbeque. He'd been to the Coopers' property years ago and witnessed the awful conditions Crazy Eddie and his sisters endured. It could drive anybody nuts. Jeremy had tried to be nice to him, but stopped after the concussion. It didn't matter—Crazy Eddie disdained the world and everybody in it.

After the last case of beer had been finished, somebody brought out a baseball bat, and then a couple of two-by-fours were pulled from under a trailer.

"Let's do this thing!" Randy shouted, swinging the two-by-four. "I'm serious."

The voices blended into a soup of noise and emotion in Jeremy's mind. "Crazy Eddie Cooper's going down." "I'll open a can of whoop-ass on him." "Going kick that boy's ass." "I'm sayin' it's us or him, you know." He didn't know who was saying what anymore. He finished his fourth beer and shouted in agreement.

Then Jeremy heard truck ignitions start and found himself squeezed in the cab of a truck with Randy and two other foul-smelling dudes heading down the highway towards the Coopers' property. Jeremy, bewildered and enthused at the beginning, began to feel an ache grow in his belly. The beers were having an effect on his usually teetotaled body, but there was something more. Cooper, as big as he was, would be slaughtered if these guys didn't back down. It was an ambush of overwhelming and unfair power.

While flying at 70 mph down a rural road, Kevin, in the lead truck, leaned out his window and gave out a long howl, like a coyote caught in an electric fence. Everybody in Jeremy's truck shouted and the truck behind them honked and flashed their lights. This was a football team ready to storm the field, rebels charging the Union line. The caravan drove for a few minutes longer, and then Kevin pulled over.

Though the windows were open in the cab of the truck, Jeremy felt overheated and nauseated. Kevin walked over and stuck his head inside.

"I think we passed it. Not sure. Any of ya'll been to Crazy Cooper's?"

Jeremy bit his lip, not wanting to say anything. Kevin walked to the other truck, asking the same question. Jeremy's mind reeled back to the third grade, the one and only time he had visited Crazy Eddie's property. It seemed like a forgotten dream.

"Nobody knows where. Really?" Kevin leaned inside the window again, his breath reeking of alcohol. He looked directly at Jeremy. "Rogers, don't you know him?"

"Yeah, I think it's a couple miles up," Jeremy said, coming back to the present. "You'll see a row of mailboxes on the right." He stopped; he didn't want to say any more.

"Which house is it? I'd hate for us to knock on the wrong door and scare some old lady."

The three guys in the cab laughed. Jeremy swallowed, trying to keep the information inside. But the intense stares, the heat, the odors, and the anticipation of those guys wanting to confront Crazy Eddie was too much. He tried to keep his mouth shut, but words came out.

"It's…it's down the dirt road for another mile or so. The Cooper house is the last one… Where the road ends."

"Alright. I knew somebody had been there. Let's do this thing."

Kevin let out a holler. Randy and the others shouted as well. The noise inside the cab was deafening.

5. LITTLE EDDIE

As the caravan sped up, Jeremy vividly recalled his only visit to Crazy Eddie's house. It was Eddie's ninth birthday party, and Jeremy didn't know how many third grade classmates were invited, but he knew some parents weren't allowing their children to go. He had sat in the passenger seat looking out the window at passing decayed houses surrounded by scraggly-yellowed weeds while his mother, Gail, navigated through a treacherous potholed dirt road. She wanted to turn around as soon as they entered the Coopers' property. The house had exposed tarpaper walls and mismatched shingles on the roof. It looked worse than anything they had passed on the way. There were at least five malnourished dogs on chains that barked incessantly. Tractors, cars, and appliances were dismantled and rusting to varying degrees all over the property.

Gail pulled to a stop and sighed. "Well, you're a good Christian boy by being friends with the less fortunate." She looked at him with wary eyes as if telling him it would be okay to go back home. Jeremy smiled, crawling out the seat with a present in hand. "I'll be back a little early to pick you up. Okay?"

"Sure," Jeremy said, shutting the door.

The dogs strained against the chains, snarling at Jeremy who clenched his teeth, trying not shiver. He had been told that you never want a dog to know you are afraid of it. He walked up to the filthy screen door and peered inside. It was dark, but he heard a television.

"Come on in," a woman yelled from inside.

Jeremy waved to his mother who was still watching from her car. She nodded and slowly crept down the road. He pulled open the screen door and found Eddie sitting in a Camaro bucket seat in front of the TV. He stared absently at static-ridden cartoons on a rabbit eared TV with the volume cranked up. He didn't acknowledge Jeremy at all. His classmates Carrie Ward and Michael Gross sat on a Buick vinyl bench against the wall, looking confused. The living room had torn lime green carpet and water-stained walls with more car seats spread around.

"Hello," Jeremy said.

"Hey," Carrie said with a nervous smile.

Jeremy sat between them.

"What's happening?"

"We're just sitting here. Eddie hasn't said anything to us," Michael said.

Jeremy looked at Eddie who hadn't moved his head an inch since he arrived. Just staring at the TV. Weird.

Jeremy looked at Carrie, who shrugged. He had known her since kindergarten. She was athletic, smart, and always cheerful with a big smile. If Jeremy had to marry anybody from Clover, he hoped it would be her. Michael was a new student from Denver. He didn't have many friends, though he tried. His problem was that he was too different: his clothes were the expensive name brands you couldn't buy at Walmart, his parents both drove Mercedes Benzes, and he was too direct, saying whatever he felt. And Eddie, who didn't have the moniker Crazy yet, was taller than anybody else his age and was usually quiet. Most kids didn't play with him at recess because there was a high probability of getting hurt.

"He hasn't said nothing at all?" Jeremy asked. Both Michael and Carrie nodded. "Hey Eddie, how is it going?"

Eddie didn't turn around. Michael and Carrie shrugged.

"He's upset cause of Daddy," a voice whispered. They turned to see a short kindergarten girl with patches on her pants and pigtailed blond hair. She had crawled to the edge of the seat from a darkened hallway. She put a finger to her lips. "Don't say anything to Eddie or he might flip his lid."

So they sat with the girl, Ashley, laying by their feet, watching cartoons until Eddie's mother, bony and tall, strode into the room and turned off the television. She wore a short sleeveless dress with a grimy apron over it. She had bruises on her arms and what looked like swelling on her cheek.

"Why don't ya'll come into the kitchen and have some cake," she said with a forced smile.

They filed behind Eddie and sat at a plywood table around a lopsided cake with four candles and smeared white icing. Two more sisters appeared and sat at the table without a word.

"You're only four years old," Michael said, laughing.

Jeremy smiled, but didn't laugh. He could tell something was amiss as Eddie shot him a glare and his sisters dropped their eyes.

"Hey, it's all the candles I could find and cigarettes would be too hard for Eddie to blow out. So why don't you just shut your trap," Eddie's mother said with a dead serious face. "Not everybody is loaded with money in this world."

Michael looked stunned, and Carrie and Jeremy glanced at each other in shock. Eddie's intense eyes narrowed at Michael, as if he wanted to kick his butt right there.

Eddie's mother walked around the table and bopped the top of Eddie's head. "Why don't you blow out the candles? You don't want this house to catch on fire, do you?"

"Shouldn't we sing happy birthday?" Carrie asked.

Eddie blew out the candles before anybody could start. The smoke wafted slowly to the top of the ceiling. For a moment it seemed everybody at the table was watching the slow, eddying gymnastics of the white apparition.

"Let's eat up. I didn't slave away like a nigger over this cake for nothing" Mrs. Cooper said.

One of Eddie's sisters laughed, but Jeremy felt as if he had been slapped in the face. That was a word you never said, ever.

Even though Jeremy thought the cake was too dry and the icing was lumpy, he ate three slices. It was still sweet, and it passed the time as everybody sat quietly. Eddie smiled for the first time when he opened his gifts: a pack of Hot Wheels from Jeremy, a superhero action figure from Michael, and a Kansas City Chiefs hat from Carrie. His sisters looked on in envy.

"Thanks," Eddie said to nobody in particular.

Jeremy sensed Eddie's mother was annoyed at something.

"Daddy should be along with your present some time today. Why don't you get back to watching your kiddy shows?"

But it was the early afternoon, and only sports were on the airwaves. So they watched golf through the electronic snow. Eddie played with the Spider-Man action hero while his sisters watched like hungry wolves. Wynona, the second oldest girl, reached out to take one of the new Hot Wheels, but Eddie grabbed her hand.

"Ouch, you're hurting me, Eddie."

"Then don't touch what ain't yours. Got it?"

She nodded, and he released her hand.

Jeremy and Carrie looked at each other, shaking their heads slightly.

"What are you two doing?" Eddie asked.

"What?" Jeremy asked innocently.

"You looked at Carrie like you we're saying something about me that wasn't nice."

Jeremy glanced at Carrie's concerned face and then back to Eddie. "I didn't say nothing, Eddie."

"If you don't like being here, then you can get the hell on outta here, ain't that right, ma?"

"What's that?" she called from the kitchen.

"If anybody thinks they are better than me they can shove it up where the sun don't shine."

Eddie's mother walked in with a cigarette between her fingers.

"Yep. You grab 'em by the back of the ears and tell 'em to hit the road Jack. And don't you let the door hit your ass on the way out."

The girls laughed, and Eddie smiled for the second time. This time it was a more empowered, satisfied grin.

"Your guests are giving you some trouble then, son?" Mrs. Cooper said, focusing a pair of accusing eyes on them.

"They're thinking they're better than me and this family," Eddie said, imitating his mother's glare.

Jeremy, Carrie, and Michael looked at each other, flushing red.

"I haven't said one word against you or your family, Eddie," Michael said. "That's just a lie."

"But you're thinking it."

"Oh yeah, this one is a little shit, I can tell. You're the worst of them," Mrs. Cooper said, pointing at Michael with her cigarette. "You all can just pack up and leave. Just go on out the door and follow the dirt road to the highway."

"That's several miles," Michael said.

"Our parents don't get here for another two hours!" Carrie said, her voice breaking on the edge of a sob.

"I knew I scheduled this party for too long." Mrs. Cooper shook her head. "Won't be doing this again."

At that moment a rusted truck careened into the front yard and braked to a skidding halt with a wide trail of dust following it. The dogs went nuts outside yelping. Jeremy felt the room grow even tenser. It was quiet for several seconds before Mrs. Cooper broke the silence.

"Look what the cat drug in."

"Should we go to our room?" Ashley asked with wide eyes.

"Not sure yet, hon," Mrs. Cooper said. "Let's see the state he's in."

All eyes looked outside the screen door, waiting for the man inside the truck to step out. He seemed to be nodding and talking to himself.

"He's in a bad way, looks like," the eldest, Naomi, said. She was a fifth grader.

The rusty truck door creaked open. One worn boot, slowly followed by another, hit the ground. A tall, lean man wearing a filthy Royals ball cap and flannel shirt, half tucked in, stood by the door of the truck, holding on to the side for support. His knees shook slightly. He reached into the truck bed and grabbed hold of something.

"Come here, son. I got something to show you," he shouted at the house.

Eddie looked at his mother, who shrugged. He walked to the door cautiously, while nervously twisting the Spider-Man action figure.

"What is it?" he called.

"Come on out here and take a look."

Eddie hesitated.

"Go on out there," Mrs. Cooper said, shooing him with one hand while taking a drag on a cigarette with the other. "You don't want to piss him off."

Eddie stepped outside. His sisters surrounded the screen door as if anticipating a fireworks show.

"What's happening?" Carrie asked Jeremy.

"I don't know," he whispered back.

Eddie shuffled up to the truck.

"Yeah?"

"I got you something?"

"What is it?"

Mr. Cooper pulled out a compound bow with a quiver full of arrows. Eddie stood only a few inches taller than the bow.

"You can shoot deer with me during bow season now."

"That's awesome," Eddie said with pure delight. Jeremy had never seen that expression on Eddie's face.

"What's that?"

"What?"

"In your back pocket."

Eddie looked at the Spider-Man peeking out of his worn jeans. "It's a present."

"A present from who? We don't have money to buy you dolls."

"It's Spider-Man. Michael gave it to me."

"Who's... Still, no boy should be playing with a doll. Not in my house."

Mr. Cooper snatched the Spider-Man. "My Daddy did this to me too when I was your age. One of the best things he done for me."

"No, Dad, no," Eddie said, reaching for it.

Mr. Cooper shoved Eddie to the ground and then dropped the Spider-Man and smashed it with his boot. Eddie looked away.

"Are those tears? Are they?" Mr. Cooper said, standing over Eddie.

"No."

"No what?"

Eddie wiped tear-streaked grime from his face. "No, sir."

"Did you see what he did to my gift?" Michael whispered to Jeremy inside the house. "That guy is nuts."

"Shhhh," Mrs. Cooper said. "You don't want him to come this way. Not how he's acting today."

"Well, come on boy, let's go shoot some targets," Mr. Cooper said. "It's your birthday ain't it?"

Eddie nodded. "I…have some friends here."

"What?"

"I have some friends over for my birthday."

"But you…I…where are they?"

"Inside the house."

Mr. Cooper shot an angry look to the house. Carrie caught her breath and stepped into Jeremy. He held her waist and thought she would step forward again, but she didn't. Mr. Cooper adjusted his posture, tucked in his shirt, and smoothed the hair under his hat.

"You need to tell me stuff like that, boy."

"But I…"

"Hush now."

Mr. Cooper stumbled towards the house. The girls scrambled back to their chairs. Mrs. Cooper crossed her arms and widened her stance, as if she were standing against a high wind. Jeremy, Carrie, and Michael looked at each other, not knowing what to do. The screen door opened, and Mr. Cooper stuck his head in.

"Howdy, ya'll. Having a good time?" he said with a big grin. The stench of alcohol wafted into the room.

The three classmates looked at each other again; were they having a good time? No, but they knew there was a correct answer.

"Sure," Jeremy said cautiously.

"We had some good cake," Michael added.

"There's cake, huh? Well I didn't know nothing about that. Darling, did you bake a cake?"

Mrs. Cooper nodded. "Mmm-hum."

"What's that?"

"Yes, I baked a cake."

"Sounds delicious. Have any left?"

"No, honey, they ate it all." She looked at her guests with accusing eyes.

Mr. Cooper balled a fist and then relaxed his fingers. "Well, I guess they're growin'." He looked at the three kids. "Why don't ya'll come out and shoot some arrows with Eddie."

They followed Mr. Cooper and Eddie out behind the house to a gully that was heaped full of garbage. Ripped trash bags full of decaying waste, broken bottles, crushed cans, waterlogged magazines, rusted metal junk, and larger appliances were crammed in the wide depression.

"This is where we usually shoot our guns, ain't it son?" Mr. Cooper said.

Eddie nodded.

"Here, hold this." He handed Eddie the bow and ventured down into the gully.

"What's he doing?" Michael asked.

"Find us something to shoot, I suppose," Jeremy said.

Jeremy and Michael wanted to touch the bow, but Eddie held it away from them. A few minutes later Mr. Cooper brought up a large misshapen chunk of grimy Styrofoam.

"Those storms blew it further than I expected." He leaned the foam chunk up next to a tree. "Ready to take your first shot, Eddie?"

"Yep," Eddie said enthusiastically.

Mr. Cooper pulled a fiberglass arrow from the quiver and put the notch of the arrow on the bowstring. "Now hold that. I gotta get something else." He sprinted down the gulley and came back up with a faded pizza box. He grabbed a broken branch and impaled the box into the Styrofoam. "There you go. Something to aim at. Like a buck or a trespasser coming through your front lawn." He laughed. "Who am I kidding? We'd blow them away with buckshot, wouldn't we?" He slapped Jeremy on the back.

"Sure," Jeremy said with a forced smile, but Mr. Cooper wasn't paying attention.

"Alright son, aim at the pizza box and pull it back."

Eddie squared up the sights and pulled as hard as he could, the string barely going back.

"Keep it steady. Come on now. Pull, goddammit, pull."

Carrie let out a gasp.

Mr. Cooper glared at her and then Jeremy and Michael. "Bible thumpers are you? Jesus, Paul, and Mary." Mr. Cooper shook his head and turned his attention back to Eddie who continued to struggle with the compound bow.

"Come on, son. You're pathetic. You can't do nothing worth nothing."

Eddie strained harder, his face turning red as beads of sweat formed around his temples.

"Give it to me. I'll show you…show you *all* how a real man shoots an arrow," Eddie's father said, reaching for the bow.

Eddie released the bowstring with the few inches of pull he had achieved. The arrow shot out ten yards before sliding into the rocks and dirt in front of the target.

"Go get that arrow you just ruined." Mr. Cooper said, grabbing the bow. While Eddie ran to fetch the arrow, he notched another arrow into it… "Y'all watch this," he said to his visitors. "I'll show you how it is done." He pulled the compound bow all the way back with a hint of effort and shouted, "Hit the deck, boy."

Eddie dove to the ground, lying as flat as possible. His eyes squeezed shut. The arrow flew above him and impaled the upper edge of the foam with a thwap sound. The shot missed the pizza box by several feet.

Carrie had grabbed Jeremy's hand. She looked at him wide-eyed, imploring him to do something. Mr. Cooper pulled back another arrow, aimed lower, and released. The arrow zoomed inches over Eddie's head, still missing the pizza box.

"Dammit, these sights are off," he said, adjusting the brass knobs on the bow. Eddie sprinted back with the arrow. He was pale and shaking slightly. Mr. Cooper peered up from the bow. "What are you doing back here with just one arrow? Go get the other two sticking in the foam."

"B…but…"

"I said, go get the other two arrows, or do you want me to tan your hide in front of your little friends?"

"I…"

"What is it? A whippin', or are you going to get me them arrows?"

Eddie stared at his father with fury and hate.

"You think you're tough, don't you, boy? Giving me a look like that." He reached for Eddie, but his son stepped back.

"I'm getting them, okay?"

"What did you say?"

"I'm getting them, sir."

Eddie dashed to the arrows. Mr. Cooper notched an arrow and aimed at Eddie as he struggled to pull the arrows out of the foam.

"Don't!" Carrie screamed.

"This is my house, and I aim at whoever I damn well please." He turned, aiming the bow at the three of them. They screamed and dove to the ground. Mr. Cooper laughed. "Little children. That's all you are. Pathetic."

He spat, dropped the bow on the ground, and walked away. Jeremy held Carrie who shook uncontrollably. Michael was crying and had a wet spot in the center of his pants. Mr. Cooper started up his truck and backed out of the drive, kicking up dirt. Eddie sauntered up with the arrows and shoved them into the quiver.

"Ya'll shouldn't have said anything. He'll be in a foul temper after he's done drinking."

"I need to go home," Carrie said.

Eddie narrowed his eyes. "It's easy for you to go home to your nice mansions and not worry about nothing." He spat on the ground exactly like his father. "You're all pathetic." He strode into his house, his head held up.

Less than an hour after the parents picked up their children from the Coopers' and the frantic phone calls that followed, the three families assembled at the Rogers' house. Michael, Carrie, and Jeremy sat on a couch while the adults surrounded them, asking questions about Eddie's birthday party. Then the parents moved into the kitchen where they deliberated for several minutes. They came back to their children with two rules: none of them were allowed to speak to Eddie, and they would never go over to his house ever again. At school on Monday, rumors circulated that Eddie's father had shot apples off their heads and killed one of the sisters. Eddie didn't say a word to them that day and very few for years afterwards. He just glared at them with brimming hate, as if they knew his dirty secret.

6. VIOLENCE

As they drove closer to the Coopers, Jeremy's stomach twisted into knots, and the nausea began to overwhelm him. He knew he was going to puke. As they turned on the dirt road, Jeremy knew he wouldn't be a part of this mob, and he felt a violent upsurge.

"Pull over. I gotta puke."

The truck hadn't completely stopped when the passengers bounded out and Jeremy tumbled head first to the ground where he hurled and heaved, wrenching out everything in his stomach, including air. A couple of minutes later he saw a circle of boots and tennis shoes.

"Looks like Rogers couldn't hold his booze down," Randy said.

There was some muffled laughter. Kevin knelt down, putting a hand on Jeremy's shoulder. "You okay?"

Jeremy shook his head. "I can't do this. Go on without me," he whispered.

"Why don't you get in the truck and rest? We'll do our thing."

Jeremy shook his head again. "No, I don't want to go. I'll walk home."

"What are you talking about? It's five miles or more."

"I can do it."

"We ain't going to do much to Crazy Eddie, you know," Kevin whispered. "Just harass him a little."

"I'm not going," Jeremy said, turning to look at Kevin in the eye.

"Suit yourself," Kevin said, rising. He addressed the group. "Looks like Jeremy doesn't have it in him—"

"Literally," somebody said.

"We're leaving him here. He wants it that way. Let's keep going. Crazy Eddie's at the end of the road. Let's show that smartass what's what."

There were more whoops and hollers as the boys piled back into their trucks. A few of them taunted Jeremy out the windows.

"Man up, Rogers."

"Wuss," Randy shouted.

Jeremy waited, still prone, watching over his shoulder at the trucks speeding down the road, kicking up dust, as their lights shrank into the distance. With a deep inhale, he stood, brushed off, and walked towards the main road. It was going to be a long walk after a long day of work, but he wasn't going to be a part of a mob. Eddie had been through too much, and he wouldn't take a beat down like other guys would. He'd be unpredictable, not giving up when he should, only to get pounded even worse.

Jeremy stepped on the paved road when he heard the first shot. It was followed by dozens more. A cold sweat broke out on Jeremy's face. He was nowhere near civilization, but he sprinted into the darkness, running as hard as he ever had. His heart thumped wildly. Something bad happened, something evil.

Jeremy staggered to the Quick 'N Go convenience store with a painful stitch in his side. He saw Shirley, a middle-aged lady who knew almost everybody in Clover, behind the register reading a magazine. He was relieved she didn't look up when he fumbled with the receiver of an outdoor telephone. He had planned to call 911, but already heard sirens in the distance. Jeremy dialed and was grateful Gary, his father, answered instead of his mother.

"Coming home? Your mother is watching the clock. Ten minutes till curfew."

"Can you pick me up at the Quick 'N Go? I don't have a ride."

There was a pause over the line. "Everything okay?"

Jeremy trembled. "Sure. Fine. Can you pick me up? But not with mom."

After another pause Gary said, "Ok, I'll be there in a couple of minutes."

Jeremy hung up, shivering in cold sweat.

Jeremy dry heaved in the shadows of darkness behind the store. He had seen a sheriff's cruiser fly past, followed by highway patrol, and then two ambulances, and knew the worst had happened. He thought of Crazy Eddie, his mother, and his sisters, all slaughtered. Maybe it was Randy or Trevor who did it. They got knocked down and retaliated with gunfire. Maybe both sides shot at each other. Several shots had been fired. Was it from the same gun or different ones? Jeremy couldn't remember the exact sounds of the popping gunfire. And when he had run down the road, he had thought he heard even more shots, or had that been a hallucination—half drunk, light headed, empty stomach—he wondered if any of his memories were valid. It seemed impossible that he had been toiling on a roof earlier in the day.

Jeremy stayed in the dark shadows. When Gary pulled up in the family Oldsmobile, Jeremy felt an urge to stay hidden, but trudged to the car.

"You have anything to do with all this commotion?" Gary asked after Jeremy buckled up.

"Sort of."

Another sheriff's cruiser flew past. Gary studied his son. "What is it? Do we need to go to the police?"

"Maybe, but not now." Jeremy held back tears. "I don't know what happened. I left before…whatever happened."

Gary waited while his son inhaled and exhaled. "Tell me what you know," he said in a soft voice. "Besides talking to the police, you need to have your story straight for your mother."

Jeremy sighed. "I didn't do anything, but I sort of did…"

*

Jeremy told Gary everything that had happened, including the beer drinking. Everything except the directions he gave to the Cooper house. That was something he couldn't tell anybody. The story was then abbreviated for Gail, not mentioning the beer.

"I told you that you're never allowed to go to the Coopers. Never." Her hands were planted on her hips.

"I got out of the truck before they got there."

"And you don't know what happened?"

"I heard a lot of gunshots. And none of those guys' trucks left."

"I told you to stay away from there. Do you ever listen?" She shook her head.

"Can it, Gail," Gary said. "He did the right thing and walked away from a bad situation before it got any worse. That's better than most boys, so give him a break."

7. CHAOS IN CLOVER

Jeremy and his parents stayed awake all night watching the local news channels in the living room. A sheriff's cruiser, haloed with red and blue flashing lights, had parked perpendicular to the dirt road, blocking the media from driving to the Coopers. On each channel reporters stood near the car, confirming that several people had been shot and rushed to the hospital, conditions unknown. The shooter, apparently, was holed up in the house. Cameras zoomed in on whirling police lights further down the road.

Cable networks picked up the story around three in the morning as "A Shooting in Clover, Kansas." Then it changed to "The Standoff in Clover" when the sheriff confirmed Crazy Eddie and his family had barricaded themselves in the house. By the middle of the morning, after the Coopers surrendered and were arrested, the total carnage was revealed: seven dead, one critically wounded. A new name was slapped on that finally stuck: "The Clover Massacre."

The shooting was the top story in America that morning. Reporters from Kansas City, Wichita, and St. Louis as well as network and cable news flocked to the town. The Clover and Shelby local police, the Kansas Bureau of Investigations, and the ATF were all there trying to figure out what had happened.

As bits and pieces of the story emerged, it seemed that the boys began their taunts when Crazy Eddie walked out with a MAC-10 and an extra clip. Though a couple of the harassers kept firearms in their trucks, they didn't use them. Reporters said that Crazy Eddie had opened fire on all of them and then walked up to each body and shot them point blank, making sure they were dead. Jeremy felt sick. He could see the boys crawling, bleeding to death, trying to hold their guts inside, when Crazy Eddie finished them off. Somehow, against all odds, Randy survived. Barely. He was on life support, having been airlifted from Emporia hospital to Kansas City General. Reporters bearing grave faces reported that he was not expected to live. Jeremy wondered "Why him? Why couldn't Kevin be the one hanging on?"

Jeremy hadn't slept all night, and in the shower his tears mixed with the soap and shampoo. He scrubbed hard under the hot water, trying to wash away his stench of what had happened. Why didn't he go home after work?

He had emails, texts, and phone calls from friends asking what he knew about the massacre. Jeremy didn't want to answer anybody.

After an untouched breakfast and a few hours of watching the news, Gary drove Jeremy to the sheriff's office in the late morning. As they crawled towards Clover's town square, traffic clogged up worse than anything Jeremy had ever seen. Not even as bad as the annual Thanksgiving night celebration, when the town spruce is lit, all of the local stores open for business, and, most importantly, Santa sits in the square's gazebo for pictures with children.

Gary parked several streets away. Clover felt surreal as they walked the five blocks to the police station. News media staked out sections of sidewalk. Countless reporters with video cameras or audio recorders covered the massacre from their designated territory. Hundreds of curious people loitered in groups watching the spectacle, and a few took pictures like Clover had the Eiffel Tower. Jeremy knew some, but more looked like strangers.

Jeremy and Gary took wide berths around the media, ignoring them when they tried to get their attention. Passing by the "citizens of Clover" who were interviewed, they heard the same mantra repeated: "Nothing like this has ever happened here."

They walked towards the Sheriff's office, a two-story gray box and probably the ugliest building in the square. A crowd surrounded the two steps in front of a podium, blocking the entrance.

"What's going on here?" Gary asked two gray haired women with matching Clover Cavalier visors and windbreakers. They looked like they could be sisters or cousins. Jeremy had seen them around, always together since he was a boy.

"Suppose to be a statement any minute now," one said.

"They've been saying that for last two hours, though," the other said in a huff.

"Doesn't look like we're going to be able to get in there," Gary muttered to Jeremy. "At least until this thing is over. Let's get something to eat."

Jeremy nodded, staying calm, but feeling fifty pounds lifting from his shoulders. He didn't have to talk to the police or anybody for now.

Jeremy and Gary crossed the square to the Main Street Café. Although it was crowded, they managed to get a booth with a view of the square. After ordering slices of pie, they watched the chaos outside silently. I caused all of this, Jeremy kept thinking.

"Crazy, ain't it?" the waitress said as she pushed a slice of Mississippi mud pie to Jeremy, breaking him out of his trance. "All these reporters and people from who knows where."

They both nodded.

"Looks like Clover's finally on the map."

"Too bad it ain't for something good," Gary said.

"But it's better than nothing, which is what we've been for a long, long time."

She sauntered to another table, refreshing their coffee. Jeremy, finally feeling an appetite, shoveled his slice away, while Gary pecked at his cherry à la mode. They ate quietly, looking out the window. Instead of the crowds lessening they grew with cameramen bearing tripods and reporters with microphones until the entire street was blocked. The waitress returned.

"I hear they still haven't started the press conference yet. I guess they're trying to figure out what to say, huh?" They nodded back to her. "Would you guys like to order anything else? If not, we've got a buncha people waiting for a table."

Jeremy looked at his father, pleading with his eyes to leave.

"No thank you, we're heading home."

Jeremy sighed with relief.

8. AFTERMATH

Jeremy never talked to the police. It seemed that they and the public knew the events before the shooting, at least the barbeque and the angry mob.

"Jeremy needs to go to the station and tell them what happened," Gail said.

"And do what? Tell the police what they already know. We'd end up with reporters up on our lawn for days, trampling on your azaleas, and labeling Jeremy something like "the lone massacre survivor" or "the lucky Clover kid" or something as stupid. Nothing good will come of it. Aren't I right, Jeremy?"

"Yes," Jeremy said quickly. He never wanted to be the center of any attention, and definitely not this. Finally Gary convinced Gail to at least sit on it until things calmed down.

Besides, the Clover Massacre took on a life of its own. The Kansas ATF found a few acres of pot growing in the back of the Cooper property, along with extreme right-wing militia propaganda and a cache of unregistered automatic and semi-automatic weapons. Mr. Pete Cooper, who claimed to be passed out drunk during the entire bloodbath, turned out be Mr. Edward Nickles from the Missouri Ozarks, wanted for a string of armed robberies and a murder twenty years earlier. The two youngest Cooper girls were shipped out to foster families far away. The eldest, Naomi, who had just turned eighteen, was arrested along with her mother for distribution of marijuana.

In town, the older people were saying that this was the biggest thing in Kansas since *In Cold Blood*. Several reporters from the coasts rolled into town, including the *Los Angeles Times*, *The New Yorker*, and *Newsweek*. Rumors circulated that Hollywood wanted to give Crazy Eddie a million dollars for the rights to his life story. Of course that sent the Clover residents into a tizzy. How could those godless liberal moviemakers give money to a mass murderer?

Jeremy kept his involvement in the massacre to himself. Although others had seen him at the barbeque, nobody was sure who left with whom. Randy was the only survivor, but he was in a deep coma. People were saying that if he survived he would be paralyzed and probably wouldn't remember much since half of his head was missing. Jeremy hoped Randy would recover to full health, but perhaps with a little forgetfulness. He didn't want to be tied to the party at all.

Whenever the phone rang, Jeremy's heart raced. Was the sheriff on the line wondering why he gave those boys directions to Crazy Eddie's? Why he ran away? Why he was keeping quiet?

9. FUNERAL

The funeral for Kevin was held at the Prairie View Methodist Church. Parishioners, relatives, and friends crammed into pews with dozens more crowding the aisles. Even though he didn't want to go, Jeremy felt that he must. Sitting with his parents and sister, Jessica, who drove out from Wichita State, he could barely hold his head up. Instead he stared at his feet, waiting for the services to be over.

L.T. Diamond, with sagging shoulders and unkempt hair, looked as if he had aged by ten years since Jeremy saw him a week earlier. Jeremy had grown up watching L.T. in awe. He had been so outwardly confident—Kevin, his only son, emulated him perfectly—but when Pastor Edwards eulogized the brief but colorful life of Kevin, L.T. let out a low moan that chilled the audience. Later, when Jeremy shook his fragile hand, desperately wanting to apologize, he saw hollow eyes in a man no longer there.

Jeremy avoided the other funerals. Though several of his friends and Jessica attended them, he couldn't swallow the idea of watching more families suffer. He felt ill and spent hours in the basement playing video games. The noises, the predictable movements, it was like medication. When insomnia struck, which was almost a nightly occurrence, he'd sneak downstairs and play until morning light.

The news media covered all of the funerals and the comings and goings of Clover residents—the IGA grocery store, the post office, and even church services. People walked briskly away from the cameras keeping their heads down. Everybody complained about the intrusive media. Then, shockingly, they were gone. Clover, it seemed, was no longer significant.

10. SCHOOL

When school started two weeks later, students were saying that Crazy Eddie—the "Crazy" prefix permanently affixed—was a part of a nihilistic separatist group like Timothy McVeigh. It seemed he had his sights set on shooting up the school to rail against institutionalized education. Good thing that those boys, God rest their souls, intervened. The boys were becoming martyrs. Jeremy kept his mouth shut and watched, with something like amused detachment, as the drunken ass has-beens turned into saints.

During third period on the first day, all classes were sent to an assembly in the gymnasium. Jeremy nodded to several friends, but he wanted to be alone. He found an end bench next to a cluster of freshmen. He sat and stared at the sandstone wall. Principal Morgan stood behind a podium under a basketball hoop, looking at notes. After everybody was seated he made his speech.

"Students, faculty, and staff, thank you for coming today."

As if we had a choice, Jeremy thought.

"Our town of Clover suffered a horrible tragedy a few weeks ago. The fallen men were Cavalier alumni. All of us probably knew one or all of the victims. Several of you are related to the deceased. It is going to be tough for some of you…some more than others, but I want you to know that we have hired extra counselors for the next two months."

Principal Morgan had three counselors stand next him. Two men and a woman. All three had sad sensitive faces and pale clammy skin. Jeremy knew he couldn't talk to any of them. They wouldn't understand. They looked like they lived in basement libraries, reading Freud or whatever psychology books were popular. They hadn't lived outside, mowing lawns, fixing roofs, playing football.

"If you need to talk about how this tragedy has affected you," the principal continued, "I truly encourage you to take advantage of their services. They are trained professionals." He then looked out at the students in the bleachers and sighed. "Please bow your heads. This might not be considered proper by some folks, but you all know it is the right thing to do." He closed his eyes. "Dear Lord God Almighty, please look down on us and give us strength to persevere through this time of tragedy. We have lost our sons, our brothers, our teammates, our classmates. We know you have a greater plan, but please look kindly on those poor boys' souls. Also, please help Randy Cochran to pull through and return to the health and happiness he once knew as a Clover Caviler. In your name we trust, amen."

The students repeated a resounding "amen." Jeremy inhaled and opened his eyes. He looked around. Some students were crying and hugging. Others held their heads down, occupying their own personal space. A few had their chins up with forced smiles, doing the Kansas stiff upper lip.

"You may return to your classes," the principal said.

A murmur grew as the students made their way down the bleacher steps. Jeremy felt relieved. He had been dreading classes and the inevitable assembly, but he had held it together. Perhaps the worst was over. He felt a tap on his shoulder and turned to see Carrie. Whenever he'd bump into her throughout the years, a spasm of happiness coursed through his veins. But today he felt a twinge of uneasiness.

"Hey Jeremy, how was your summer?" Her eyes were red, but she smiled beautifully.

"Brutal. I mowed lawns and did some roofs."

Carrie's expression changed. "Did you work with Kevin?"

Jeremy nodded. "I did. I was with him the day he got shot."

"Holy crap." She grabbed his hand. "You should see one of the therapists they brought here."

"I don't need that," Jeremy said, jerking his hand away. "I mean, I wasn't shot at, you know. I didn't see anything. Nothing at all." Jeremy took a breath. This was ridiculous. He felt like he was being accused even though he knew better. It was Carrie after all. He had never known a purer heart.

Carrie's empathetic brown eyes mixed with hurt and curiosity studied Jeremy. Her empty hand remained open where she had held his.

She said, "I can't help thinking about how Crazy Eddie never liked us since—"

"That birthday party." Jeremy completed her sentence. Carrie smiled at him. Good God, she was gorgeous, Jeremy thought. He then felt a surge of panic as they stood staring at each other for a moment too long. "Yeah, I uh… I see why he's a nut case and all with that screwed up family, but he needs to take it out on his dad, not us."

The school bell rang. Carrie nodded.

"Where you going now?" she asked.

"Geometry. And you?"

"Trig."

"That's right, advanced track."

"Yep, AP calculus next year. Maybe calc two at Emporia College my senior year."

"That's awesome. My goal is to keep good grades, you know."

"You will," she said with another radiant smile. "It was great talking to you, Jeremy."

"You too."

He stood watching her walk out of the gym until Matt Hendershot slapped him on the back.

"Rogers, what's up, brotha? Saw you talking to Carrie. She's really gotten hot all of sudden. Who knew?"

"Yeah. How are you, Matt?"

"School sucks. And it's the first day."

They walked back to their classes, Matt talking and Jeremy nodding, but not listening. His mind was fixated on Carrie.

11. THE CALM BEFORE

A week after the reporters left, Clover felt emptier than it ever had. The vacant lots, unoccupied parking spots, and lonely cafe booths reinforced a notion of insignificance. Even the spaces between buildings seemed wider. But without the outsiders around and extra time to absorb the tragedy, citizens seemed freer to voice differing opinions. A few asked why the boys were up on the property to begin with, and, besides Kevin Diamond, weren't most of them known troublemakers? But it was usually an aside, as most conversations concerned Randy Cochran's health and the evilness of Crazy Eddie. Jeremy, like everybody in Clover, prayed for Randy's recovery; however, he included the caveat of memory loss.

Jeremy felt he held a dirty secret that nobody had figured out yet. Why had he given those idiots directions? Why didn't he keep his mouth shut? The boys had been hell-bent on finding Crazy Eddie, and most likely would have, he tried to rationalize. It wasn't my fault, he kept telling himself, wanting to believe, but finding it hollow.

A preliminary hearing was held in Paola to determine whether Crazy Eddie would be tried as a minor or not. Reports came back to Clover saying that Crazy Eddie was cuffed to his chair after threatening to kill his public defender at the hearing. He was declared an adult and would be tried in a full courtroom. A trial date was set in eight months. As the weeks led to months, anticipation grew. Would Crazy Eddie freak out in the courtroom? Would Randy come out of his coma? How quick could the jury sentence Crazy Eddie to death?

The reporters came back to Clover for the trial in late April with a vengeance. It seemed as if they had doubled in numbers. Although there was an uneasy feeling, most of the citizens were privately glad that they were back. The eerie stillness they had left last time was unnerving.

For Jeremy, the past eight months had gone from bad to worse. He'd been able to maintain passing grades and socialize during the fall, but he found himself caring less about grades and increasingly wanting to be alone. He hated Friday and Saturday nights because of the pressure: pressure to attend parties and talk to people. Group dynamics—everybody in agreement concerning inane issues or idiots staking out dumbass opinions to get a rise out of others—unnerved him. He'd rather be in the basement playing video games in his own mind space that he didn't have to share. When he turned sixteen, Jeremy bought a used Ford Ranger. Besides driving to school, it became a vehicle of escape. He could run home or leave the house, cruising on random rural roads past vast empty fields or parking by a creek and watching the mucky waters flow. As the trial got closer, Jeremy's grades dipped to barely passing and insomnia hit. Three hours of sleep was a good night. He felt lucky that his name had not been mentioned in any way regarding the massacre…yet.

PART 2

THE TRIAL

12. SLEEPLESS

Jeremy did not sleep the night before the trial. He felt certain that he would be taken by police officers to the courthouse and forced to testify that he led the boys to Crazy Eddie's so that boy-giant could slaughter them. Tossing and turning, Jeremy's heart raced in panic. He clenched his teeth and dug his fingers into his pillow. When another surge of adrenaline hit, he jolted upright, taking deep breathes. He tried not to think about the trial, desperately tried not to think of anything at all except for breathing.

Eventually, Jeremy's heart rate settled, and he closed his eyes, starting to drift off. Suddenly his heart would seize up and pump like crazy. This happened all night long. He wanted to tell his parents he was having a heart attack, but going to an emergency room meant attention and questions. He didn't want that. Not if he could help it.

After five in the morning, Jeremy managed to fall asleep. Then his cell phone rang. He jumped in a panic. They were coming for him. Did the prosecution need another witness to testify, or did defense want him to say the murders weren't Crazy Eddie's fault? One or the other. Dear citizens of Clover, Jeremy Rogers, a high school sophomore and the lawnmower man, led your sons to a massacre.

Jeremy found his pants ringing on the floor. He dug through the pockets and pulled out his phone. To his relief, it was Carrie. Why so early?

"What are you up to?" she asked in a cheery voice.

"Sleeping. Or trying to. What's up?"

"You wanna see the trial today?"

"What?"

"The trial. I'm standing in line with about fifty other people."

"What about school tomorrow…or today, I mean?"

"Skip it. Besides, a bunch of us are here. We're all going to get in trouble. But, we can argue this is a learning experience you can't get in school."

The last place Jeremy wanted to be was in the courthouse. He didn't want somebody pointing at him and shouting, "He's the one."

"I don't know."

"Come on Jeremy. Do it for me. Puleeze?"

Jeremy felt his heart flitter, but differently.

"What about Michelle?" he asked. She was Carrie's best friend and biggest rival. They seemed to do everything together except when they were fighting. Although she was physically hot, Jeremy saw Michelle as dense and shallow.

"She's here…with Zack." Her voice dropped in tone when she mentioned her more than once ex-boyfriend. She didn't need to elaborate. "Can you be here with me, Jeremy? I'd really appreciate it."

Jeremy sighed. How could he say no?

13. WAITING

By the time Jeremy penned a note saying he had to be at school early and left the house, a line of people circled the courthouse. Sunlight had yet to break. Jeremy recognized almost everybody. They ranged from middle-schoolers to the gray hairs. He joined Carrie near the front of the line. She gave him a hug and an unexpected kiss on the cheek.

"Can you believe all of the folks who showed up to this?" She seemed incredibly happy to see him.

"Not this early. Anybody heard of sleep?" Jeremy said with a smile.

"Looks like you haven't got any yourself," Carrie said, reaching for his face. He flinched.

"I'm fine. Just restless." He wanted to change the topic. "How long have people been here?"

"Some spent the night here, like those folks," she said, pointing to a couple sitting on folding lawn chairs inside sleeping bags pulled up to their chins.

"Who are they?"

"Don't know. Might be Crazy Eddie's people or maybe just some curious folks from out of town."

Jeremy spotted Michelle Anders and Zack Utley up ahead. They held each other closely around the waist. He also noticed a few important people were missing.

"I don't see L.T. Diamond or any of those boys' families."

"I don't think they have to stand in line. It's like a VIP thing."

Feeling pressure creep into his chest, Jeremy exhaled. He didn't want be around the families if he could help it. "I don't get it. So why do you want to be here? It'll be on the news tonight."

"What do you mean, you don't get it? This is history, right here, in Clover freaking Kansas. It's something I can tell my children and grandchildren about, you know. It's like that OJ Simpson thing. But it's our generation's big event, at least here, and what's even crazier is that we knew everybody involved."

Jeremy nodded, but felt irritated by Carrie. Didn't she see this was an awful phenomenon? There was lightheartedness amongst most of the people standing in line, as if there were waiting for a movie on a Friday night in Emporia. He'd already heard more than once from different voices, "I wonder if Crazy Eddie will be any bigger" and "They're going to fry him."

Carrie nudged Jeremy. "Penny for your thoughts. You seem to be deep in your head."

"I keep thinking about Crazy Eddie's birthday party. Can't shake it."

She searched his eyes, as if trying to gauge whether she was supposed to laugh at Crazy Eddie's past or be morose.

"What's gotten into you? You've pretty much disappeared since the massacre. You didn't see the counselors, did you?"

Jeremy shook his head.

"You've got to get it out of your system. Those murders were awful, but you got to keep moving. I cried for two days straight when I heard about it, you know. I was sick with grief. But then it was out of my system. I'm here to watch the trial and see that Crazy Eddie gets what he deserves. I think watching the trial might help you."

She stared at Jeremy until he had to turn away. "Suppose you're right," he mumbled.

She squeezed his arm. "Maybe you should see a counselor."

Jeremy stiffened. "I don't need to see anybody. I think I'm just sleepy, that's all." He forced a smile. "Thanks for saving me a place in line. This will be fun."

14. OPENING DAY

A little before eight, courthouse officials arrived, shaking their heads in disbelief. The line stretched for two blocks down Main Street.

"You know we can't fit all of you in," a security guard told the crowd with a chuckle.

"Never seen anything like this in my life, never," an older clerk said loudly to a younger colleague as they walked by Carrie and Jeremy.

"Never been anything like this, you old coot," Carrie muttered to Jeremy.

Two sheriff deputies had been circling the area all night in their patrol cars and a new pair replaced them in the morning. A hush flowed through the crowd when the county correctional van passed by and parked in back of the courthouse. The sheriff's cruiser followed close behind.

"Did you see him?" several people asked out loud.

"I hope he makes a run for it and Sheriff Hensley shoots him dead," somebody said to the chuckles of others.

A handful of junior high kids ran to the back of the courthouse and then came back minutes later to spread the news. They had seen Crazy Eddie. And he was bigger and meaner than ever before, according to Timmy Lynch.

"He was wa...wea...wearing orange and had a bunch of tattoos."

"He's got a shaved head too," Gregg Anders added.

Jeremy and Carrie saw Crazy Eddie an hour later. They were in the first group of sixty to be seated. When Crazy Eddie was brought out, it seemed like his already enormous physical body had grown even more since his arrest. His bulging muscles seemed to have doubled in size. As reported, he had tattoos running all over his arms and it looked like the bottom of a swastika peeked under a sleeve of his orange jumpsuit. He kept his shaved head down, but carried a savage scowl. "No remorse," Jeremy heard whispered behind him.

More people were let into the courtroom until it was standing room only. There had been rumors about who was on the jury. Everybody knew somebody, but some of the talk was obviously wrong since many of the names bandied around were sitting in the audience. When the door opened for the jury box, it seemed there was just as much excitement to see who they were as there had been to see Crazy Eddie. Walking in first was Thomas Ginty. A staunch outspoken conservative with bumper sticker slogans on his truck to prove it. He walked to the jury box, trying to stare down Crazy Eddie.

"Since Mr. Ginty is on the jury, Crazy Eddie will hang for sure," somebody said.

But when librarian Edna White, physics teacher Ralph Newton, and Presbyterian minister Ronald Edwards entered, the tone in the room changed.

"Edwards, he's a liberal minister," the first voice said.

"All three of them are," another person said.

"They're not all ministers," Carrie said, causing a slight chuckle around her.

The rest of jury included Jessup Cotton, a retired farmer; Anne Fischer, a sewing shop owner; Hailey Granger, a tax accountant; homemaker Cynthia Garrison; and Janelle Hughes, a single mother who worked part-time at the IGA grocery store.

The bailiff told everybody to stand, and Judge Roy Rhinehart entered. He was a short, round man, and known to be jovial when not wearing the robe, but in the courtroom he wore a stern frown.

"Be seated," he said as he eased into his chair. He looked around and exhaled. "This is the most people we've ever had in this courtroom in the history of Clover. I'm only going to say this once: any outburst and I will throw all of you out here. I might even throw in a contempt of court charge to the loudmouth. This is serious business here, and we have several weeks up ahead, so sit tight and be quiet."

He then turned his attention to the lawyers and talked in legal jargon that Jeremy knew only bits and pieces of from TV. The prosecution was led by Carson McKinney, a balding man in his late forties who had made an unsuccessful run in the Republican primaries for state Attorney General. Everybody knew him from the ads and billboards from his campaign. Ever since he became lead prosecutor on the case, he had been on the radio, TV, and papers discussing the case.

Carson kicked off the opening arguments detailing the savagery that the accused "Mr. Eddie Cooper" had committed when killing fine upstanding young men of Clover. He asked the jurors to consider the families that lost their sons to such a heartless murderer and to give them the justice that was rightfully theirs. Crazy Eddie didn't help himself either, staring cold hateful looks at Carson.

"The evidence will show that this is not a case of accidental homicide, ladies and gentlemen, but rather of a wicked and sadistic man without remorse or conscious, who committed the most heinous crime in the history of Clover. You must find Eddie Cooper guilty of first-degree murder not only for the victims' families, but also for the citizens of Clover and all of Kansas. We cannot as a society have a man like Eddie walking the streets ever again."

Carson walked back to his table with a half-cocked, self-satisfied smile.

The defense was led by Lawrence Elliot, a young man who had graduated from the University of Kansas School of Law a few years earlier and was rumored to be a card carrying ACLU member. Who else but an ACLU freak would want to free a killer? Crazy Eddie had been given a couple of public defenders, but had refused to cooperate with them. Then Lawrence stepped up out the blue and took the case pro bono. He declared to the media that "a travesty of justice was happening" and he was going "to salvage what I can and make sure that Eddie Copper gets the best representation possible." In a baffling twist, he had demanded that the trial be held in Clover instead of Paola as originally scheduled.

People in Clover initially scoffed at the twenty-seven year old upstart trying to take on a seasoned prosecutor like Carson McKinney. But when Lawrence stood for his opening argument, some women in the audience leaned forward with rapt attentiveness they neglected to give Carson. Jeremy noticed Carrie's longing look. Lawrence was tall and handsome. His trim body was accentuated in a tailor-cut suit. Where Carson came across as salt of the earth, Lawrence had a debonair confidence unknown to Clover. Even before he opened his mouth, Jeremy hated him.

Lawrence argued that Crazy Eddie was at home fast asleep, when he was awakened by a rowdy bunch of boys looking for him. "Yes, perhaps they came from good families, unlike Eddie's own background, but at that moment in time, those boys were drunk and hell-bent on hurting young Eddie.

"Please keep in mind that although he is large, Eddie Cooper was only fifteen years old at the time of this incident. How was he supposed to know that, according to the prosecution, those young men, whose average age was twenty-two, weren't intending to do any harm? Alcohol was found in all the deceased bodies. If you look at the criminal records of the deceased, all except one had been charged with either drunken driving or assault and battery, and in some cases both. Yes, the acts that Mr. Cooper did may seem heinous, but take a step back and consider that Eddie was scared for his life." He let the last word linger.

"Imagine a gang of seven drunk and rowdy adults calling out your name on your property in the middle of night. You're in a house full of women, and your father is passed out drunk. What would you do? Seriously, ladies and gentlemen, what would you do? You would do like any proper Kansan would do and defend yourself and your property. That's for certain. And I ask you, what was the intent of those young men who drove onto the Cooper's *private property*? Honestly, we do not know. We can only speculate, as the prosecution has done. Randall Cochran is the only witness who knows the original intent of his colleagues. He knows the reason why they decided to antagonize

Mr. Eddie Cooper on his property and what they intended to do when they encountered him. Nothing that the prosecution says can be substantiated by any eye witnesses except for Mr. Cochran, who is currently in a coma, and the Cooper family, whose house those men descended upon in the middle of the night."

Lawrence turned and sat down. Jeremy swallowed hard. Carrie gave him a nudge.

"Are you okay? You look as white as a ghost."

"I think I need some air. It's stuffy in here."

As if the judge were listening, he banged the gavel and called for an early lunch break. He said it was "too hot and humid with all these bodies in here."

15. UNAVOIDABLE

The springtime air, while fresh, didn't clear Jeremy's nausea. He sat on a park bench, trembling.

"You want me to get you some water or something?" Carrie asked.

"No, I think I just need to head on home…or to school."

"You were close to Kevin, weren't you? I've seen how the massacre has affected you. You haven't been the same." She put her hand on his knee.

"It's not that. I mean, I knew him from church and did some roofing jobs with him, but… I remember the party before they went after Crazy Eddie."

"You were there!"

"Shhh. Not so loud." Jeremy looked around at people milling around.

"Did you tell anybody?"

"I don't have anything to add. At least nothing that would help Kevin's family or the others."

"What did they want to do?"

Jeremy shrugged. "They wanted to kick Crazy Eddie's ass. They really had it in for him. Especially Trevor."

Carrie nodded. The ex-quarterback's could've-would've-if-not-for-Crazy-Eddie excuses were well known. "I understand why you don't want to talk to anybody, but…" she squeezed his knee and looked into his eyes. "You should see a counselor."

Jeremy felt panicked. Did he tell Carrie too much? He couldn't tell anybody the whole story. Not if he wanted to keep living in Clover.

"Carrie. Jeremy."

Carrie yanked her hand off Jeremy's knee. Zack walked up with Michelle following behind. Zack gave a sly smile while Michelle stared sourly at Carrie, as if telegraphing "he's mine bitch" to Carrie.

"What are you guys up to?" Zack asked. He had his thumbs hooked into the back of his faded blue jeans, like he was trying to mimic Kevin's swagger.

"Oh, we're just…" Carrie began.

"I think I'm coming down with the flu," Jeremy said, standing. "I'm going home."

"You don't look…" Carrie started, but then read Jeremy's pleading eyes. "Sorry I dragged you here."

"It's okay. I just need to rest. I'll get over it."

"Later, man," Zack said. "Thanks for keeping us safe."

Jeremy stopped, frozen. "What?"

"From germs, dude."

Jeremy nodded and walked to his truck.

*

Jeremy lay in his bed, knowing that he should try to avoid the trial as much as he could. Why did he have to be the one who knew where the Coopers lived? His brain spun into a piercing headache.

Jeremy stayed in bed the next few days with a minor fever. He didn't go to the trial or to school and didn't want to hear anything about them. He wanted to be alone and have the world go on without him. But in the idle moments of silence in his mind, even if he was listening to heavy metal on his headphones, he desperately needed to know what was happening.

Carrie and other friends emailed and texted up-to-the-minute details from the courthouse. Because of the constant crowds and truancies, the judge would allow broadcasts "against his better judgment" the following week. Lawrence Eliot was being called "Lawrence from Lawrence"—home of the University of Kansas Jayhawks and where he lived. It seemed that Lawrence was more persuasive than Carson, tearing down the prosecution's arguments, and even had the people of Clover wondering about the true intentions of the boys. When L.T. Diamond gave testimony about the pureness and unlimited potential of his son, Lawrence was able to be sympathetic and skillfully ask questions about his son's character. Through L.T.'s testimony, Lawrence painted Kevin as a tough fighter—winning most of the scrapes during his life—and a natural leader. He even got L.T. to admit that his son would have had the guts to lead a posse after somebody like Crazy Eddie.

People speculated nonstop about what the jury members were thinking. Supposedly Lawrence made eye contact with all the women in the jury box, even making the librarian Edna White blush more than once. It was reported that the men in the box, especially Thomas Ginty and Joseph Cotton, seemed to have a look of consternation whenever Lawrence spoke.

Carson did his best to shake Lawrence's charm by showing the jury horrific pictures of the massacre during the county coroner's testimony. Edna reacted most visibly in horror, while Janelle Hughes reportedly smirked when she saw the photos. All of the men in the jury did their stoic best to look unaffected.

On Friday, Jeremy's mother declared that he didn't have a fever and had to go school, nerves or not. Jeremy found several empty chairs in his classes, and everybody only seemed to talk about the trial.

"So how's the trial?" Mrs. Patterson asked Jeremy in his English class.

"I only saw part of it on Monday, but I've been sick the rest of the week."

"Uh-huh," the teacher said, rolling her eyes. The half-full class laughed.

In Jeremy's third hour history class, cell phones began ringing. The teacher, baseball coach Bob Howard, turned on his radio to a news station to confirm if the rumors the students heard were true. The class waited impatiently between commercials and a national talk show jockey's rants about the moral corruption of America when he was finally cut off by a special news report. It was true. Randy Cochran had come out of his coma.

16. RANDY

Clover was buzzing more than ever. What would Randy say? Could he remember anything at all? He had, after all, been shot twice in the chest and once in the face. It was a miracle that he even survived.

The next day, the news reported that Randy was fully conscious and remembered the shooting. Carson McKinney moved to have the trial delayed until it was known whether Randy could testify. Lawrence argued that the case should continue unheeded, but his charm wasn't strong enough to convince the judge. The trial was put on hold for a week for doctors to determine whether Randy would be capable of testifying. After the doctors said it might be possible, the trial was delayed for another week for the prosecution and defense to depose him. Doctors and nurses watched and could stop a session at any moment.

By the third week, doctors said that if Randy wanted to testify he could, but for limited periods of time. He did, and arrangements were made for an ambulance from the University of Kansas Hospital to drive Randy back and forth from the trial. Almost a month after he awoke, the trial was set to resume.

Jeremy had lost considerable weight during that time, and his already low grades plummeted. He could not focus, and his appetite waned. He was on edge, jumping at any noise, expecting to hear his name called out.

The morning the trial was set to resume, Jeremy and his parents sat at the breakfast table. He picked at his bacon while his parents watched the morning news from the TV on the counter. A blonde reporter stood by an ambulance outside of the Kansas City hospital.

"Randy Cochran was loaded inside this ambulance just moments ago and is expected to give testimony in Clover against Eddie Cooper for the slayings of seven young men," she said with a plastered smile. "Randy's recovery is miraculous and unprecedented as far as I know in the state of Kansas."

Jeremy felt acid swirling inside his stomach. He couldn't eat another bite.

"You look awful," Gail said. "Aren't you getting enough sleep?"

"I'm fine."

"No you're not, and you're hardly eating. Haven't even touched your eggs. What's the matter?"

"Nothing."

"It doesn't look like nothing. Should I call a doctor?"

"Leave him alone," Gary said with a concerned look in his eye. "And turn off that television. It makes me nervous."

Jeremy was relieved, but as he walked out to his truck, his father followed him.

"Anything you need to talk about?" Gary said in a firm voice.

"No, nothing," Jeremy said. He tried to look his dad in the eye, but he couldn't, focusing on his chin instead.

"Maybe we should've talked to the sheriff. I dunno."

"It's okay. Probably be worse if I had."

Gary nodded. "Well, this trial will be over eventually. Hopefully you'll get back to normal."

"Yeah, hopefully," Jeremy said and got into his truck.

17. THE TESTIMONY

A TV was brought into Jeremy's first hour classroom, and neighboring classes piled in. The class sat riveted as a large male nurse wheeled Randy, strapped to a wheelchair and equipped with a breathing apparatus, to the front of the courtroom. Jeremy felt sick. He wouldn't have been able to recognize Randy. Diamond's premier roofer had lost weight, looking skeletal instead of chubby. His head was shaved and the left side of his face looked pink and swollen. Randy's left eyelid seemed permanently shut. He feebly put his hand on the bible and in a concentrated and slow raspy whisper promised to tell the entire truth.

Lawrence stood and asked for a private meeting with the judge and the prosecutor before the questions began. They left Randy sitting on the stand alone for ten minutes. The cameras stayed on him as he sat at the bench, staring forward and looking small and scared, blinking his one good eye.

Jeremy had to look away and doodled nervous circles on a notebook for three pages. His classmates were mumbling, impatient, wanting the trial to begin.

"I thought Lawrence from Lawrence was cool," a girl spoke up.

"That douche is holding everything up," her friend said.

"Lawrence is a tool," a jock said.

When the trial started up again, Carson asked Randy to recall what had happened on the night of the shooting.

"Why did you go to the Coopers' property?" the prosecutor asked.

Randy concentrated hard for a moment. The classroom was so still, like nobody was breathing, Jeremy thought.

"We just wanted to put Crazy, err, Eddie Cooper in his place because he had already been causing trouble with many of us."

"When you say causing trouble, what do you mean?"

"Well, he uh…had broken Trevor, uh, Trevor Mc… I'm sorry, I can't remember things too well."

"That's fine, you're doing well, son."

"Well, he'd broken last year's quarterback's arm, and had beat the livin' shi…tar out another fella in Shelby." Randy looked confused for several seconds trying to recall something. "He'd also knocked somebody out…who was there at the party…"

Jeremy's blood chilled while Randy's seemed to be searching fragments of memories for his name. Finally Randy shook his head.

"I forget now who it was."

Jeremy exhaled. He couldn't believe that Randy forgot about him, and hoped it stayed that way.

"That's okay. We get the picture. You had said that you were going to put Eddie Cooper in his place. What did that mean?" Carson asked.

"Nothing much really… I, I'd been put in my place years ago."

"What happened back then? When you were put in your place."

Randy smiled slightly as if he was reliving the moment.

"It was just some rough-housing. Nothing unbearable. Guys pushed me around and called me names. I just manned up and took it. Had beers with them later."

"Were you planning to do the same thing to Eddie Cooper?"

Randy leaned forward slowly. "Yes, sir. Ab…Absolutely."

Jeremy felt the sting of a lie. Maybe Kevin would have had mercy on Crazy Eddie if had he stepped out of the house unarmed, but not Trevor or the other boys. They only had bloodlust on their minds.

"Tell us what happened next. After you decided to put Mr. Cooper in his place."

"Well…as I remember, we loaded up and drove up to his place."

"When you say we, do you mean you and all of the victims on the night of August thirteenth?"

Jeremy gripped the edge of his desk and clenched his jaw.

"Yes, sir."

Jeremy sighed, relief overwhelming him. He wasn't sure if he could make it through the testimony. He could tell he was flushed, but nobody in the classroom noticed. They were all transfixed on Randy's testimony.

"So you just drove up to Mr. Cooper's house. What happened?"

"We, uh… We got lost at first, and then somebody knew where he lived, so we drove there."

Jeremy couldn't believe his luck.

"Then what?"

"Um…" Randy looked to be thinking hard. "We, uh, got out of our trucks and called out his name…and…" Randy's body began to shake. "Then a-a-all hell broke loose."

Randy broke down into tears, his body quaking. The male nurse walked up to the stand, but Randy pushed him away.

"If you're able too, could you give us the...details of what happened?"

Randy took a moment to collect himself. "I don't know, sir... I-I remember getting out of a truck... Kevin was already out and calling Crazy... I mean Eddie's name... The door to the house opened..." Randy exhaled, his good eye staring at the floor. "Before I knew what was h-happening, a machine gun blasted us all to hell."

"What happened to you then?" Carson asked.

"I got blown backwards... I, um...crawled under my truck." Randy paused, wiping a tear away. "I heard more blasts.... Sh-sh-shouting and screaming from everybody... Then quiet, but only a few seconds wh...when he started shooting again..." Randy's body trembled. "I, uh, I don't know what happened after that... I passed out."

"So Eddie Cooper reloaded and shot everybody else?"

"Objection," Lawrence said. "He's leading the witness."

"I'll rephrase, Your Honor. Did Eddie Cooper shoot all of the men you were with after they were already wounded?"

"Yes, sir. He did."

"How can you be certain? You said you passed out."

"Well, I did, but not before...he, E...Eddie walked up to K...Kevin and...shhhhoot him in the head."

A collective gasp went through the classroom. Jeremy felt the bottom of his stomach drop.

"Did Eddie Cooper say anything?" Carson asked.

"No, sir. Not Eddie…bu…but Kevin did. He, uh, beg…begged him not to shoot. Sssss-said it was a misunderstanding…then boom." Randy choked up, allowing tears to slide down his cheek.

Somebody from the gallery yelled, "Murderer! You murdered my son in cold blood, you son of a bitch." The cameras panned to L.T. pointing an accusatory finger at Crazy Eddie.

The judge banged his gavel. "Somebody take Mr. Diamond out the courtroom now."

"You're a murderer, Eddie Cooper! Blood is on your hands!" L.T. shouted. His voice broke as a deacon and a sheriff's deputy grabbed and escorted him to the doors. Crazy Eddie turned to stare at L.T. A camera zoomed in on his face. It was cold and unmoving.

"He's a killer. Look at those eyes," somebody in the back of Jeremy's class said.

Judge Reinhardt said, "Members of the jury, please disregard that outburst. You must weigh all of the evidence from the testimony here. If a sentencing occurs, then we may take testimony from Mr. Diamond. Until then, I repeat, please disregard what just happened. Please continue, Mr. McKinney."

The prosecutor stood with a solemn face. "Seeing how fragile the health Randy is in, I'd better cut this short. No further questions, Your Honor," Carson said, sitting down.

Lawrence stood up, took a breath, and walked over to Randy. "I understand you aren't feeling too well these days." The audience and classroom gasped at the insensitive comment, but Randy chuckled, shaking his head. Tension in the classroom eased.

"I… I've been better."

"You are very lucky to be alive, and I think we can say all of Clover's prayers were answered when you pulled through a few weeks ago."

"Thank you…sir."

"You know, I have to ask you these questions. It's my job, and everybody gets a defense in America." Randy nodded slightly. Lawrence dropped his sensitive expression, replacing it with a confused look. "I understand you want to protect your fallen buddies, but did you guys think Eddie'd come out and greet you with cookies or something when you hollered out his name?"

"Objection," Carson said.

"I'll rephrase. Mr. Cochran, what did you plan to do once you got to the Cooper's residence?"

"It's, uh, kind of, uh…sort of like, um…" Randy searched for the word in his head. "A tradition. You, uh, show up at somebody's doorstep…tell 'em to come out."

"Does this strategy often work?"

"Yes, sir. It does…"

"What happened if you don't walk outside?"

"Well, uh, if you don't…you're considered a…um, a…um…" Randy looked up at the ceiling, looking genuinely stumped. "I can't think of a proper word to use in public."

"Are you thinking of a word like 'wimp?'" Lawrence said.

"Yes, wimp."

"But you don't use that word? Wimp?"

"Not…not anymore… Used it in elementary school."

"Does that other word start with a 'p' and describe a woman's body part or a cat?"

"Objection, what is the relevance of this?" Carson said.

"I'm trying to create an atmosphere of the event of what happened and the state and mood of these men on the night of the attack, Your Honor," Lawrence said.

"Objection overruled."

"Is it the 'p' word?"

Randy cracked a slight smile. "That's the one."

"Pussy, correct?"

The classroom burst in laugher.

"Objection!" Carson shouted, standing up suddenly and knocking over a pile papers. "This is irrelevant and it is being broadcast live to families and children, Your Honor."

"Withdrawn, Your Honor," Lawrence said, hiding a smirk.

The Judge nodded. "Continue. I don't need to instruct the jury."

Lawrence from Lawrence turned back to Randy and pasted a big smile on his lips. "Mr. Cochran, Would ever want to be called that p-word?"

"Never... Definitely not to your face... You, you'd have to do something about it if somebody called you that to your face."

A slight laugh rumbled in the courtroom.

"Damn straight," the jock said in the classroom.

"It's a code. A man code, is the right, Mr. Cochran?" Lawrence said.

"Yes sir. It is."

"So if men come taunting you to come out of the house, lest you be called that other word for a wimp, you'd have to step outside and take whatever that group is dishing out?"

"Yes, sir."

"You didn't expect Eddie to come out shooting, did you?"

"No, sir... Not at all."

"Have you ever encountered guns when you've tried to put somebody in their place?"

Randy thought about for a while, then his face brightened.

"Once, I think. A mother…maybe a sister…came out with a shotgun. Only time I recall."

"Did she pull the trigger?"

"No…and Crazy Eddie didn't give no warning shot." He stared straight at Crazy Eddie. The camera switched to Crazy Eddie holding his stare.

"I didn't ask about Mr. Cooper," Lawrence said. "But that's fine. Did you know you were on private property when you drove up to the Coopers' residence?"

"It's r-r-rural… I didn't know. We s-s-stayed on the dirt road," Randy said with a determined look on his face.

"Did it occur to you that the road and everything around it might be private property?"

"No… Not at all."

"Were you drunk at the time of the shooting?"

"I… I'd been drinking some…but not drunk."

"I'm not trying to contradict you, but earlier in the trial, the coroner testified that his autopsy report showed all of the men who were killed had a blood alcohol content of point one two or higher. It sounds like you and your buddies kicked back more than a couple of brews, isn't that true?"

Randy didn't say anything, but stared down, swallowing hard.

"How many did you drink, Mr. Cochran?"

"I... I don't remember..."

"Fair enough. Can you say that you were drunk enough to perhaps not have the best idea at that moment and time what was private property or not?"

Randy dropped his chin to his chest. "I...don't know," the witness whispered.

"When Eddie saw all of you out on his front lawn, drunk by the legal definition in the State of Kansas, you did not expect him to want to defend his family's home?"

"Objection!" Carson said, rising from his chair. "This is pure speculation."

"I'll withdraw the question, Your Honor."

"Move to strike."

"So stricken." The judge turned to the unseen jury and instructed them to disregard Lawrence's last question.

Jeremy watched the students in his class as they pondered the implications of drunken hooligans invading their property so they could beat the crap out of them.

"Mr. Elliot," Judge Reinhardt continued. "I'd advise you to save your comments about the case until the closing remarks."

"Yes, Your Honor. I have no more questions."

Carson asked for a redirect, but the judge shook his head.

"After lunch, Mr. McKinney. My stomach is churning."

He hammered the gavel, and the audience rose to exit as voices increased from a cacophony of mumbles to chorus of fragmented voices. The bits and fragments of conversations that Jeremy caught over the television included phrases like "they shouldn't have been driving at all, drunk like that," "they should have known better than to enter another man's property," and "drunk as a skunk." The students sat uncomfortably silent, as if wanting to be loyal to one of their own, but feeling Randy might have been wrong.

18. HISTORY LESSON

Although Carson tried for damage control with his redirect of Randy emphasizing Crazy Eddie's violence, it looked desperate. Randy came across as guilty and regretful. Public opinion swayed in Lawrence's favor. The death penalty no longer seemed like a slam-dunk, though manslaughter—in a self-defense plea—couldn't be attained, not with Crazy Eddie's brutality.

Jeremy, in spite of himself, followed the trial obsessively. He didn't talk about it, but listened to the news, friends, or anybody vocalizing a theory about what would happen next. Even though he felt he wouldn't be called on at this point, he couldn't get his mind off of the trial. Would Crazy Eddie be freed or fried? He honestly didn't know and felt too scared to have his own opinion, lest it might come true. And he felt he had done enough dirty work arranging the fates.

Lawrence from Lawrence brought in folks from Topeka and the University of Kansas to discuss property law and defending it. He even had an old historian and rancher, Dr. Jake Clemmons, discuss the history of Kansas and what happened to cattle rustlers and other ne'er-do-wells who entered another man's property a century ago.

"Branding, blinding, hanging, dragging a man by his ankles with a horse to the county line. They did a lot of things to men who entered another man's property with ill intent," Dr. Clemmons said. He was dressed in a faded jean shirt with pearl buttons and a turquoise stone bolo. His seventy-year-old skin was leathery from decades in the sun.

"Did these trespassers know that they were going to get into a heap of…" Lawrence stopped himself with a self-deprecating smile. "Let me rephrase that. I'm getting a little caught up in all this exciting history." The audience laughed. So did Jeremy's classmates. Can't they see this is just an act? Jeremy thought.

"Did they know they were going to endure all of this retribution if they entered another man's property illegally?" Lawrence continued.

"Yep. It was a code. A code of the property owner you might say. If you entered another man's property you were a dead man until you made it back to other side of that property line."

"Was there much documentation on these procedures?" Lawrence asked.

"Well, nothing was officially documented, you see. It was something that was just done. Outside of a few hangings and an occasional write-up in a town paper by an editor, most documentation is found in diaries of old."

"Would you say that what Eddie Cooper did was in keeping with code of the property owner?"

"Well it was a bit of an extreme…"

"But was it within the bounds of property owner code from the olden days?"

"Yes, I'd say it was, but with modern technology."

A chill went through the classroom. Jeremy knew what they felt because he was feeling it too. Crazy Eddie might've been right.

19. CAUGHT

More than once Carson had called for a sidebar with the judge and Lawrence. It seemed that the prosecution wanted to cut a deal, something that would have been unthinkable a week earlier. For almost eight months people had talked with dead certainty about how Crazy Eddie was going to get a state funded lethal concoction shot in his veins. No two ways about it. But then Lawrence rode into and shook everything up. Left was right, and up was down. Was it possible that Crazy Eddie was a victim and not a mass murderer? Jeremy was as confused as everybody else.

After the property rights experts testified, constitutional law professors discussed the importance of the second amendment. It seemed like Crazy Eddie was only defending his family from a group of hooligans with uncertain intentions. More than one Clover resident admitted to spending a night tossing and turning, trying to figure what was right and what was wrong. Rumor had it that Lawrence wasn't interested in cutting any deal: manslaughter or nothing. Even with all the arguments supporting Crazy Eddie, people said a manslaughter charge just wasn't enough. He had killed seven unarmed boys, finishing them off at point blank range. And Carson McKinney had to know that no district attorney with an ounce of political ambition or any modicum of self-esteem would allow such a compromise.

Lawrence finished his expert testimonials with psychoanalysts and doctors, all of whom testified that Eddie Cooper had suffered from posttraumatic stress disorder from an abusive father and ridicule of his family by the students and citizens of Clover. Most of the accused citizens, whether sitting on the wooden benches of the courthouse, relaxing in the comfort of their sofas, or watching from molded plastic classroom chairs, kept their eyes down, focused on the floor. Jeremy could tell that Lawrence's guilt trip on Clover was having an effect. It seemed that people believed they may have had something to do with the creation of the monster they named Crazy Eddie. Lawrence had momentum, and the slam-dunk murder charge seemed to have slipped away from Carson. Then Thursday night happened.

Ladies had been swooning over the handsome and sophisticated Lawrence Eliot since he had arrived in Clover. He had taken up weekday residence in a Holiday Inn in Emporia instead of commuting daily from Lawrence. His equally polished law school friends often drove down to Clover to visit and watch the trial. In the evenings, Lawrence and his entourage hung out at Chuck's Bar and Grill on the Shelby-Clover border, drink a few pints of beer before dinner and then downing stronger stuff afterwards. Ladies of all ages and marital statuses had ventured up to the group and sometimes Lawrence or his crew would buy them a shot or two. More than one man had threatened to kick Lawrence's ass because a girlfriend had swooned or shared a drink with him. Even though Lawrence flirted with women at the bar, the biggest rumor wasn't about them. It was about those who couldn't get in the bar.

Jeremy heard Lawrence's name paired with a few high school girls. All of them had reputations of easy virtue and had most likely been with men over eighteen long before Lawrence came to Clover. But when a state trooper pulled a BMW over for erratic driving at two in the morning, what he found, according to local buzz, was Mr. Lawrence Eliot with his pants unzipped, an open bottle of scotch, and fifteen-year-old Katie Brannegan.

20. LAWRENCE

The trial was delayed that Friday morning until the following Monday, based on "outside developments." Gossip hit the fan and splattered far and wide. Phone calls, emails, texts, and social networking pages buzzed with stories of horn dog Lawrence and how he had swept the virtuous Katie Brannegan, granddaughter of a Baptist minister, no less, off her feet with his wily lawyerly ways.

The charges against him included driving under the influence, reckless driving, endangerment of a minor, lewd exposure to a minor, statutory rape, and sodomy. Lawrence made bail early Friday morning, avoiding most of the reporters by ducking his head under his jacket, and jumping into a drinking buddy's Land Rover. Reporters and hecklers followed the SUV to his hotel in Emporia. Lawrence sprinted inside and returned with bags in hand a minute later to the waiting Rover. Fewer followed him back to Lawrence, where he finally escaped them via underground parking in an exclusive townhome. Within hours a video of Lawrence running back and forth with the press following him was sped up and cut to Benny Hill music. Jeremy laughed longer and harder than he ever remembered in his life.

*

Lawrence surprised everybody in Clover when he attended services on Sunday at the Prairie View Methodist church. He arrived sullen. His shoulders were sagging and his face held a world of sadness. But his public display of contrition seemed to backfire. Jeremy sensed the congregation's discomfort. Lawrence sat on a pew with space on both sides of him, like he had a contagious disease. Few people shook his hands afterwards, though several children gawked, and many parents physically pushed their young daughters away from him.

*

On Monday, the crowd that surrounded the courthouse was even bigger than when the trial began, or for even Randy's testimony. People from the neighboring towns came over, including that annoying roving Westboro Baptist church notorious for protesting soldiers' funerals. They could have made a case about God hating pedophiles, but kept with their anti-homosexual message instead.

Katie's parents and immediate relatives locked the doors to their houses and refused to talk to anybody. They had circled the wagons around Katie.

Jeremy watched Lawrence on TV when he arrived at the courthouse all smiles with an extra helping of smarmy charm, but Jeremy saw fear in his eyes. The courtroom sounded like a football stadium with nonstop chattering voices. Even when the judge strode out, the audience did not quiet down. Judge Rhinehart banged his gavel so hard it looked like the handle cracked.

"I'll throw every one of you out if I hear another peep. This is a courtroom, my courtroom!" He was red faced, and the veins in his temples pulsed rapidly. "You all are guests here and nothing more."

The judge looked at Lawrence wearily for a moment. The camera switched to Crazy Eddie, who flexed his tattooed fingers back and forth, giving the judge a contemptuous stare. The camera returned to Judge Rhinehart as he turned to the jury. "I don't know what the hell you've heard, but it doesn't matter at all. This case is solely about Mr. Eddie Cooper and nobody else."

He turned back to Lawrence.

"Now, Mr. Elliot, would you like to continue from where you left off on Thursday?"

"Thank you, Your Honor. I would."

The camera took a shot of Crazy Eddie staring straight ahead and not even acknowledging Lawrence. It seemed like his chances for manslaughter were as thin as the day he was arrested.

21. WYNONA

On Monday afternoon Lawrence brought out his final witness: Eddie's sister, Wynona. Maybe he was banking on her testimony to sow doubt in the jurors' minds. But when she sauntered up to the stand in a short black skirt and ill-fitting high heels, Jeremy could tell even through the television that Lawrence lost hope. During the swearing in, she chewed gum while her polished neon-pink nails touched the bible. After the judge had her spit out the gum, she described the fear she felt on that night.

"When those boys showed up, drunk and all, shouting and cursing at Eddie, I was scared. We all were."

"How did your brother take all of the threats shouted at him?"

"Poor Eddie didn't know what to do. He was trying to defend the family property. And they were standing right there in the middle of it."

"Some have been saying that it was too much, what Eddie did. Do you believe it was too much?"

"You have seven or eight twenty-year-olds showing up in trucks in the middle of the night, shouting and making noise. Who isn't going to overreact, you know? I mean, they were the ones who attacked us first. They were the ones who trespassed."

Carson was gentle with Wynona, though he managed to paint her as a conspirator in the massacre after she admitted to previously "being with" a couple of the boys.

"I definitely didn't like them, not the way they treated me after…"

"After what, Miss Cooper?"

"After I gave them something better than they'd ever had before."

Laughter erupted from the audience and in the classroom. Crazy Eddie stood and glared at the audience.

"Ya'll better shut up. You hear?" he said in a deep voice.

Lawrence put his hand on Crazy Eddie's shoulder.

"Now just sit and—"

Crazy Eddie shoved Lawrence to the floor. He glared, standing over his lawyer.

The audience gasped. Everybody in Jeremy's classroom stood to watch closer. Two sheriff deputies grabbed Crazy Eddie and tried to set him back into his chair. Even though he had on cuffs, he pushed and kicked them away. Lawrence got up and tried to help hold Crazy Eddie down as he struggled, swearing and bucking. Lawrence caught an elbow in the mouth and fell to the floor a second time. The audience was in an uproar, standing on their feet and blocking the television cameras.

*

"Sit down!" students in Jeremy's class yelled at the TV.

Although nobody could see her, Wynona was yelling, "Eddie, Eddie!"

The judge banged the gavel. "Order, order!" The handle broke off of the gavel.

The deputies tased Crazy Eddie three times before he went down.

"I want him out of here, now!"

The deputies dragged Crazy Eddie out the back door. People in the audience were on their feet, some taking pictures with their cell phones. Lawrence, pale and shaking, pulled out a handkerchief and dabbed blood from his lip.

"Sit! Everybody!" the judge yelled, slamming the broken gavel down. Reluctantly the audience sat down. Reinhardt surveyed the room. "Mr. Elliot, are you okay? Can you continue or do you need another delay?"

Lawrence seemed to be considering several things, but said "I'm fine, Your Honor."

"Mr. McKinney, you may proceed so we can get this…" The judge stopped for a moment as if holding back a profanity. "This case over with."

Carson stood. "Absolutely, Your Honor." His chin was up and shoulders drawn back as if he had some rooster in him.

"Excuse me," Wynona said, talking into the microphone. A black mass of tear-streaked mascara surrounded her eyes. "I just want to make it clear that I didn't want those boys to be killed or nothing, okay? I just didn't like a couple of 'em. That's all."

The judge looked as if he wanted to strangle the witness.

"I have nothing more, Your Honor," Carson said quickly.

"Recross, Mr. Elliot?" the judge asked.

Lawrence stood, and smoothed rumpled his suit. He looked exhausted. "No, Your Honor, the defense rests."

The judge turned to Wynona. "Please leave the booth immediately and don't say another word."

She gave him a severe look and strutted out of the courtroom with a defiant sway in her hips. Judge Rhinehart reddened with anger.

22. ALL THE DIFFERENCE

Tuesday brought closing arguments, with Carson talking in the morning and pushing for a guilty verdict on the capital murder charge. Crazy Eddie sat with his hands and feet in shackles. Again, he gave almost no expression except for the same glare maintained throughout the trial.

Carson reminded the jury of all the forensic evidence he had presented earlier, as well as the unknown potential of the dead young men whose lives were "violently snatched away from us." Then he painstakingly recounted all of the major statements his witnesses had made. It almost put Jeremy to sleep.

"These murders became premeditated once Mr. Cooper reloaded his automatic weapon on those unarmed boys, and by definition of Kansas state law…" Carson said, holding up a piece of paper dramatically. "I quote, by the *killing of more than one person as part of the same act*, Mr. Eddie Cooper has fit the circumstances required for capital murder.

"Remember, seven young souls perished in Clover that night, not because of property rights or any second amendment argument. We all know if he had shot his gun in the air those boys would have been running home. This was cold-blooded murder. He shot those defenseless boys while they lay wounded on the ground. This man deserves nothing less than death, ladies and gentlemen. He is a cold-blooded murderer."

After lunch, Lawrence, looking fresher and more energized than the previous day, reminded the jury that not only was Eddie sixteen, "but he was sleeping in his house on private property when a caravan of drunken men showed up with the idea of giving him a beating. Did he overreact? Most certainly. But did he start this? Absolutely not. It would have been considered self-defense a century ago, and there is no reason it shouldn't be today. He stepped forward to defend his family, and any red-blooded American with an ounce of spine in his backbone would have done the same. Eddie Cooper did not knock on their doors and shoot them. Not at all. Those eight men trespassed on a man's private property, looking to cause at minimum mischief, and most likely bodily harm, and that, ladies and gentlemen, makes all the difference."

23. VERDICT

The jury deliberated for almost two weeks. It seemed that all of Clover was on pins and needles, waiting for the verdict. Rumors abounded that the jury was deadlocked because Jessup Cotton wanted a capital murder charge and nothing less, or that Janelle Hughes demanded that Crazy Eddie be freed, but the most popular one was that Thomas Ginty was delaying as long as possible so that he wouldn't have to go back to repairing the roads.

Lawrence was living in Lawrence again, an hour and a half away from Clover. He was on call if the jury was ready to announce their verdict. The only other reason for him to come back to Clover was for his post-indictment arraignment a month later when he would enter a plea.

Jeremy was restlessly ambivalent. Crazy Eddie shouldn't have been harassed by those boys on his lawn, but he shouldn't have shot them all to hell either. He was glad it would be over soon, regardless of the outcome, and maybe could he get back to being who he once was.

Jeremy was in fifth hour biology, drifting in lazy daydreams of sleep—what it would be like to have solid dreamless sleep—when cell phones that were supposed to be off started vibrating. The jury announced they had reached a verdict. Mr. Howard turned on the radio in time to hear Judge Rhinehart delay the reading of the verdict until the morning, "considering all the travel of key people involved in this case, including the defendant Mr. Cooper from the Emporia detention facility."

Minutes later, Principal Morgan spoke over the intercom cancelling the next day's classes. "It'll probably be a zoo tomorrow in Clover, so I recommend all students stay at home, if possible."

He wasn't wrong. The streets by the courthouse were full of local gawkers, those from Shelby and Emporia and even a few from Missouri and Oklahoma. All of the Kansas City and Wichita news stations arrived to cover the story. Jeremy stood in the crowd with Carrie and most of their classmates. When Lawrence drove up in his black BMW, silence trickled through the crowd. It was not the respectful kind of silence though—more like a mass revulsion after seeing a notorious war criminal.

"That's the bad one isn't it, Mommy?" a little girl said a little too loudly, creating a domino effect of chuckles.

"You bet it is," somebody called from the crowd.

Lawrence glared disdainfully at the girl and marched into the courthouse.

"I guess he'll be on trial next," somebody said.

"Naw, a guy like that gets a plea bargain and cleans up the road for a week. He ain't ever going to be coming back here again," an older man said.

"Good riddance, scumbag," another voice said.

Although most people, not even considering Crazy Eddie, were wishing the worst for Lawrence, journalists were saying that the jury's nearly two-week deliberation should make him feel confident. It meant a lack of unity. Most likely somebody or somebodies didn't want to convict Eddie Cooper of first-degree homicide.

Judge Rhinehart had cleared the courtroom except for immediate family members of the murdered and Wynona. He also had the TV and radio broadcast banished. Hundreds stood outside the doors waiting to hear the verdict.

Jeremy and Carrie stood shoulder to shoulder, the tips of their fingers almost touching. Jeremy felt electricity rocketing through his body. He wanted to grab her hand, mesh his fingers between hers. But he couldn't. His throat was Sahara dry and his body was stiff: he couldn't move or speak. She didn't say a word either and seemed as rigid as they waited. He watched birds returning from the winter, jumping from budding branch to branch. Jeremy decided he was going to touch Carrie, put his arm around her and point to a blue jay hopping in a nearby rosebud when the doors of the courthouse flew open. L.T. and his wife strode out.

"What happened?" somebody yelled.

"Bull crap is what happened. A huge steaming pile of it. There is no justice in America anymore."

"L.T.," his wife chided.

"Bull crap!"

Other family members of the murdered piled out of the courtroom looking equally disgusted.

The jury found Eddie guilty of having illegal weapons, misuse of a firearm, and failure to call the authorities, but not guilty of first-degree murder. As the jurors revealed later, they felt the charge was too high. They would have voted for manslaughter or even a lesser murder charge, but Carson didn't give them that option. There had been a fifty-fifty split, but eventually it became apparent that even as heinous and cold-hearted as the massacre was, those boys had stepped on private property and should have known better. It was as if some idiot went to the zoo and jumped in a lion's cage. You don't fault the animal when it tears that person apart; you fault the stupid human.

Jeremy wasn't sure if he was let down or not. He was glad that Crazy Eddie would be serving time, but not a life sentence—even though a freed Crazy Eddie could only lead to more trouble. It seemed the town of Clover, however, was disappointed. Quietly the masses walked back to their cars saying very few words above a murmur. Jeremy and Carrie walked back to their cars silently. Jeremy wasn't thinking about the verdict, but was trying to find the words to ask Carrie out. He saw himself confidently asking "Hey, are you doing anything tomorrow?" or straight to the point: "Would you like to go out?" When he looked at Carrie, however, he noticed her eyes weren't on him, but Zack and Michelle walking hand-in-hand. Jeremy felt the urge to get home and play video games.

The sentencing trial happened the next week, and the judge took the jury's recommendations, giving Crazy Eddie the maximum time possible with a ten-year sentence. It was reported that Crazy Eddie wasn't happy, swearing at Lawrence as deputies pulled him away in cuffs. Carson had been on the television and radio stations denouncing "the gross miscarriage of justice in Clover," though nobody cared what he said. He let Clover down. Lawrence had slipped away unnoticed, probably happy to be out of Clover.

PART 3

HIGH SCHOOL

24. LIFE CONTINUES

Jeremy continued his life almost the same way as before the trial, before the massacre. Smiling and getting along with people, he was good at that. He didn't think that anything stood out noticeably, but he had changed. He felt hollow. Sometimes when he shut his eyes at night, he would drop into an instant free-fall, his body hurtling into a dark abyss. He'd wake with his heart racing and teeth clenched. He would then play video games into the morning, completely exhausted.

Lawrence Elliot from Lawrence came back to Clover for his own trial. As predicted, he turned everything upside down and mixed and muddled everything until he was convicted on a couple of misdemeanors and given commuted sentence. He had to perform community service, but it wasn't even picking up trash. He gave talks about the dangers of driving drunk and provided legal advice at community shelters. The girl's family changed their position from wanting to prosecute and designate Lawrence as a pedophile to publishing a statement that nothing had happened in his car that night; only a simple misunderstanding.

L.T. Diamond dropped out of the church and atrophied into an embittered hermit that even his wife could no longer reach. Jeremy was grateful L.T. didn't attend his church anymore. Any reminders, whether sisters, brothers, or parents of the dead boys, or even those damn Diamond Contractors signs, could turn a decent mood into a downer.

Jeremy's conversations with friends stayed on temporary and trivial subjects, avoiding any deep topics. He also found video games to be infinitely more intriguing than homework or people. Although he talked to Carrie often, the ease and comfortableness he had with her over the years were gone. He began to feel nervous around her. She had started dating a jock in the class ahead. Although it didn't look like anything more serious than hand holding and kissing, it made Jeremy depressed, wanting to fall inward.

In the cafeteria, he had slowly migrated away from "The Table" where Carrie, Zack Utley, Matt Hendershot, Michelle Anders, and all of the cool kids ate to tables of lesser distinction. To be at the cool kids' table you had to be quick on your feet, as jabs were thrown in rapid machine-gun fire, but with constant respect given to the kings and queens lest they turn their wrath and that of others against you. Zack was an asshole of the highest order who seemed to work hard at it, like it was an obligation because he was the popular guy. He had money, looks, and played quarterback, centerfield, and guard in the three sports that mattered in Kansas—football, baseball, and basketball. He wore his letterman's jacket almost every day except for the hottest ones. He exuded outward displays of confidence, except when looking into his eyes after he made a boastful comment that was unfounded in reality or common sense. Behind those eyes were layers of fear and insecurity.

To Jeremy, it seemed Zack still wanted Carrie even when he was with Michelle or some other girl. They had dated in middle school and again for a short time before the trial. It was almost as if Carrie had no choice—she was destined to be with him.

Jeremy had hated Zack since the eighth grade, when Jeremy stood alone at a urinal doing nature's business. Out of the blue, Zack unzipped and stood next to him, even though there was another toilet a spot away he should have used according to man code edicts.

"Hey Rogers, you know when I made out with Carrie, I got to feel up her boobs. They are sweet."

Jeremy nodded, feeling emotions of envy, embarrassment for Carrie, and anger at Zack's arrogance. He loved Carrie and would have given a couple of fingers just to make out with her. Boob touching wouldn't even be on his agenda…unless it was okay with her.

Zack's eyes watched Jeremy carefully, waiting for a reaction. He was gauging Jeremy, but for what?

"Why are you telling me this, man?" Jeremy said with a flush and zip up.

"What do you mean? Just letting you know that I got some. You're close to her. Did you ever get any?"

"Boob?"

"Yeah." The truth of the matter was that they did kiss and hold hands a few times in preschool up until first grade, when it wasn't cool for boys and girls to be together.

"No, not yet."

"Not yet sounds like never to me, bro. I've had her already, but you better jump on her before somebody takes her away. That is, unless you're into dudes."

"Shut up, man."

Zack laughed. Forced and dumb.

*

Jeremy hung out with friends four tables down whom he had forsaken a few years earlier to be cool. He said hello to everybody at the cool tables—there weren't hostilities, he just no longer played football or kept the edge needed to be there. He sat with Erik, Graham, Cynthia, and Lisa. They were academically motivated and had aspirations for college.

"How about you?" Erik, a scrawny bespectacled sixteen-year-old asked. "Do you know where you want to go to school?"

Jeremy shrugged. "Don't know yet. I need to make sure I get through high school."

The table laughed and Jeremy smiled, but he really meant it.

25. SAM

Somewhere during the middle of the trial, Jeremy stopped losing weight and started gaining it. As he grew in height, so did his waistline. He'd been big boned and might have even been called thick before, but a tummy started to creep over his belt. It would have been called a beer gut, but in reality Dr. Pepper and snacks from plastic bags were the culprits.

"If that belly grows any more you won't be able to see your toes. You need to get out and exercise," his mother would chide. But upon hearing the word exercise, Jeremy recoiled, desiring the comfort of his bed.

*

When the school year ended and as the summer progressed, Jeremy got leaner and tan mowing lawns and working on a few roofs here and there. Like his stint in football, he was second string. Only if somebody else was sick or injured—injuries usually happening after work, in a bar or a house party, though it would be reported as a workplace injury for the workers' comp—would Jeremy work on a roof. The roofers drank in the name of comfort after a day of back straining labor. Jeremy joined a few times, but the déjà vu was too strong. He began declining invitations, instead going straight home to the comfort of the basement.

*

A month into his junior year, Jeremy's sister, Jessica, brought her boyfriend Sam over from Wichita State. His handshake was so firm that it seemed like he was intentionally trying to break fingers. He was hyper-optimistic and assured, pursuing a Business Administration degree. He had played a year of baseball at Wichita State until he had to "retire" after tweaking his knee sliding into second base.

"Could've signed with the Reds out of high school, but went for the scholarship instead. At least now I'll have a solid business degree. No injury can take that away."

Jessica and her mother sat almost star struck listening to the one semester college athlete talk between bites of Gail's homemade lasagna. Jeremy, his hand still smarting, wasn't impressed. He looked over at his father, who also seemed underwhelmed. Sam came across as a blowhard, like so many other males that women desired. He couldn't understand it. Couldn't they see past the ego and the veneer of big talk? Carrie didn't. That's why she dated morons like Zack.

"Isn't he great, mom?" Jessica asked.

She nodded as if lacking words.

"So what about you, sport? Do you play anything?"

It took Jeremy a couple of seconds to realize Sam was talking to him.

"Oh, uh…no. Used to play football, but I got a concussion," Jeremy said, upset that he felt like he was apologizing.

"It was from Crazy Eddie Cooper, that psycho who killed all my friends. Remember?" Jessica said.

"Yeah, that guy was crazy," Sam said.

"I wouldn't allow Jeremy to play football after that," Gail said.

"So what about other sports? How about playing baseball or something?"

"Naw. I'm getting by fine. Football was my sport."

"And getting fat," his sister added.

"Hey," Gary said. "Leave your brother a little dignity. He drives a mean riding lawn mower in the summer."

The table laughed. Jeremy sat quietly stewing. There wasn't another sport he could play. He couldn't hit a fastball to save his life, he was too short for basketball, and there was no way he would even consider cross-country. It hurt that his father was ganging up against him.

A rift had been developing between Jeremy and Gary since the trial. People had been laid off at the power company, and though Gary had kept his job, he worked more hours with a pay cut. When he came home, Gail would gripe about Jeremy's low grades and lack of motivation. He and Jeremy had a few talks that revolved around moving forward. "The trial is over. They never called on you to testify. Consider yourself lucky and move on." Jeremy always nodded, saying he would.

"You got to buck up, kid. Get back up on that horse again," Sam said, bringing Jeremy back to the present.

"My name is Jeremy," he said, feeling blood rise to his cheeks.

"Okay, Jeremy, even if it isn't athletics, look into doing other things, like me. I got injured, but I'm still making the most of my college scholarship, you know. I'm vice president of the University Business Club and I'm in a bunch of other organizations. You should look into groups like Future Business Leaders of America or the Debate Club."

"Oh, Sam," Jeremy's mother said. "Jeremy ain't the academic kind. His grades have gotten to be something awful."

"I'd like to see Jeremy in drama. Can you see him quoting Shakespeare?" Jessica said, laughing.

"How about chess club?" his mother added before ripping into a snort of laughter.

Jeremy brought up a brave, singular smile. Let the laughs rain down, he thought, I can take it.

*

Jeremy tossed in bed, mulling things over in his mind. Was he a loser? He definitely wasn't a "winner," but then again he knew many others who were a lot worse off living in trailer parks, or those who were plain dead. He had survived by some weird combination of good luck and intuition. If that intuition didn't care whether or not he went to college or had high grades, who was to say he wasn't on the right track? Or maybe, he thought as he plunged into the darkness of his mind, he had used up his last good luck pass and was existing on borrowed time until a comet or a plane would smack him down. Lord knew he deserved it.

26. MR. SIMS

Jeremy's downward academic trajectory continued through his junior year. In the winter he was pulled from history class to the counseling office. Mr. Mark Sims, a thin bald man who wore colors of dirt and prairie, sat behind a metal desk. On top of his desk he had a manila folder open with what looked like grades, and behind him was a wall full of certificates and degrees. Jeremy read one that said *Students with Special Needs Training Certificate of Completion.*

"Jeremy, I called you in to make sure that everything is going okay."

Jeremy looked around and nodded. "Sure, everything is fine."

"Jeremy, you know your grades are suffering. I looked back at your files and, while you weren't a straight A student, you had a high B average. Of course, that was before last year and this year." He had a concerned expression that looked like pain. Jeremy tried to smile back. "I also looked at your past yearbook pictures and it seems to me you've been putting on a few pounds over the years. Not that that is necessarily a bad thing, but it could be a sign of something else. So let me ask you, Jeremy, is there anything you want to talk about?"

"No, not really."

"Not really? Does that mean there is something?" He said in a soft voice full of so much sensitivity that Jeremy felt creeped out.

"Nothing at all. Absolutely." Jeremy tried to look Mr. Sims in the eyes, but he couldn't hold his stare.

"I noticed that you didn't seek counseling after the murders a couple of years ago. Not that we had many come, but there were a few and the counseling was confidential. For those who did come…it helped them to cope with the tragedy that affected us all." He paused for a long moment. "Jeremy, would you like to talk about the murders?"

"Seriously, I'm fine Mr. Sims. Maybe a little distracted, but…" Jeremy felt his face turn red.

"Distracted by what, Jeremy?" He leaned forward, resting his chin on his knuckles.

Jeremy wanted to run out of the office. Was he sweating? He felt like it.

"You know, life and…stuff."

"I don't know, Jeremy. Please explain."

"I can't explain. It's nothing. I just want to go back to my class so my grades don't get any worse." Jeremy felt stupid for letting his voice rise.

Mr. Sims looked at Jeremy for several uncomfortably long seconds, not moving or saying anything. Jeremy squirmed. What was he expecting him to do? What was he trying to find? There was no way that he would know that he gave the directions to Crazy Eddie's house. No freaking way. Even if Randy remembered, he wouldn't have told this counselor.

"I feel… I almost want to say I know, but that would be presumptive, wouldn't it? I believe you are holding something back, something that is eating at you, and I want you to know that you can talk about it with me. You have complete confidentiality here."

Jeremy smiled with a skeptical upturned lip. He knew better than that and emphasized the point with crossed arms.

"Well okay, almost complete confidentiality. If you plan to harm anybody or yourself or commit criminal actions, I have to report it. It's the law, but what I'm saying is that it is not healthy to hold on to things. I'd like you to talk to me if you could. I've been trained in handling student interactions and have a master's degree in counseling, but if you'd like to talk to somebody else I can have that arranged, or if you could talk to somebody at your church or some other place, that is better than holding it in. Trust me. You hold something inside too long it will tear you apart and sap your energy away. You don't want that. Nobody does."

Jeremy nodded. It made sense, but Mr. Sims was wrong. He could hold it in longer. Much longer.

He was strong enough. Nobody needed to know, because nobody knew anything about it anyway. The directions Jeremy gave were known only to him and somewhere in Randy's shrapnelled brain. Everything was fine. Perfectly fine.

"I'm good, Mr. Sims, really." He held a smile for as long as he could, hoping it looked sincere enough.

27. KCCC

Early into the school year the Kansas Community College program announced a new satellite campus in Clover. They broke ground days after buying the land. This caused a little bit of a celebration: Clover was big enough to have its own college. Although there were only two buildings and a parking lot, the campus sat on twenty acres and could expand. Instead of just ROTC recruiting on campus, representatives from KCC talked to high school classes, telling students who weren't sure if college was right for them to try KCC.

What Jeremy didn't like about KCC planting a campus in town was that his mother, who had given up hope that he would go to college, now believed her son might get a degree. An associate degree was good enough.

Jeremy maintained C minus scores, either because there were always a few imbeciles in every class or teachers liked him enough so that he barely passed with a minimal amount of effort. Again he mowed lawns during the summer, but did fewer roofing jobs because there were other kids hungrier for work. He had made new "friends" playing *World of Warcraft*, *Tour of Duty,* and other online games where combinations of teams were necessary. Sometimes if he wasn't too careful controlling his subconscious, he'd imagine that he and his team of players from around the globe were the Clover boys sneaking up on the Coopers' house. Whether shooting Nazis or hacking up orcs with an axe, for a moment he'd think of Crazy Eddie and exact revenge on his ass.

His senior year began with the same low grades. Jeremy was called into Mr. Sims' office again.

"Hello, Jeremy. How are you?"

He shrugged. "Okay, you know."

"You know why you are here?"

"Grades?"

"Yes. They are quite low. You might be in danger of not graduating."

That was news to Jeremy. Sure he wasn't trying, but were they that bad?

"How are things at home?"

"Fine. No problems."

"Hmmm." Mr. Sims leaned forward with wide eyes and an open expression. Jeremy felt the creepiness again.

"I just want to graduate, you know," Jeremy said, mumbling. "I don't need a scholarship. I just want to get my diploma and move on."

"College?"

"Don't think so."

"What about KCCC opening up?"

"My mom wants me to go, so I may not have too much say about it."

"Any idea at all what you want to do for a career?"

Jeremy shook his head. "I'll look for work. I can do just about anything."

"But you won't get hired to do many things unless you have a degree."

"Most of the things I don't want to do require a degree."

"So you know what you don't want to do, but do you have any idea what you want?"

The first image that popped in Jeremy's head was Carrie, but he threw it out. She'd made up with Zack over the summer, and they were going strong. He drew a blank.

"Jeremy," Mr. Sims said, bringing him out of his trance. "Is there anything at all that you want?"

Jeremy shook his head. "No sir, I guess not."

"But you want to graduate?"

"Yes, I do. I'd feel pretty stupid spending all my time here and not making it to the end."

"Well," Mr. Sims said with a sigh. "At least you've got a goal."

"It seems I do."

28. PROM

Jeremy managed to keep passing grades through his senior year. Then a wave of anxiety hit. It was a four-letter word: prom. He felt he could ask a couple of girls, but really didn't want to. What he wanted to do more than anything else was to dig a hole, jump in, let prom happen, then crawl back out, graduate, and be done with all of it. Girls seemed to talk about it nonstop, and dudes discussed renting tuxes.

"Who you asking? Cynthia or Lisa?" Erik asked Jeremy, with Graham hovering nearby.

"Neither."

They both had smiles of relief. Jeremy understood: they wouldn't have to fight over one girl now.

"You aren't going to ask Carrie out, are you?" Graham asked.

"No, I just don't want to go."

"You heard that Carrie broke up with Zack the other day?" Erik asked.

Jeremy felt his throat catch. He hadn't heard, but nodded as if he did.

"Yeah, sure."

"You guys have been close for years," Graham said. "If I had a shot at Carrie, I'd take it."

"Me too," Erik added enthusiastically.

Jeremy smiled to himself. He didn't want to go to prom. He didn't deserve it. His goal had been to just graduate and get out. But if Carrie was available for the prom...

He saw Carrie the next afternoon walking to her car. Not that he planned on seeing her, though he *happened* to park his Ranger next to her Buick. Her eyes were bloodshot, and her eyelids were heavy.

"Hey, Carrie."

She looked up, startled for a second.

"Hey, Jeremy," she said with a smile of relief. "I'm heading home. I don't really want to talk now."

"Is everything okay?"

"Yes, it's..." then she shook her head. It wasn't okay. She looked at him, biting her lip. "It's stupid. Zack cheated on me, again. Right before prom. He says..." she bit her lip again. "He says he's got to get some...some action because if I don't give him any, he can't help himself. He says it's a male thing. Is that true?"

Jeremy's mouth dropped open. It was true he had urges, strong urges he tried his best to ignore and often took care of in the shower. But he also knew that deep in his heart that he would wait and be the absolute most chaste monk in the world rather than pressure Carrie.

She put her hand on his chest. He stiffened.

"I don't mean to put you on the spot talking about personal issues. I guess I needed to vent a little, you know. You're a good friend, Jeremy. You really are." She stood up on her tiptoes and kissed his cheek. "Thank you."

As Carrie drove away, Jeremy stood unmoved, realizing he was tomato red. Why hadn't he said anything to her? What about prom? Had she made a decision based on his silence and blushing? What was it?

*

Carrie and Zack were back as a couple the next day, and it seemed that Zack had an extra swagger in his step. Jeremy made sure Zack wasn't around before he stood at a urinal. Even though Jeremy knew, he didn't want to know. The couples' names were on the ballot for prom king and queen, and they were expected to win. Jeremy made his intentions known loud and clear to anybody who asked: he was not going to prom.

29. PROM NIGHT

The week of prom, Jeremy fell into a depression. The hysteria, the immaturity, the emphasis on one temporary event that was supposed to define the time of your life seemed so incredibly stupid. It took extraordinary effort to get out of bed, and on Saturday he stayed under the covers, barely able to move. He turned off his phone and unplugged his computer. That evening, Jeremy had supper in bed, and when his parents had settled into a movie on TV, he snuck out the back door.

He had a destination in mind, though he wouldn't name it. He didn't want to attract his parents' attention by starting up his truck so he walked, one foot in front of the other, for almost two miles. The hike relieved some of the tension that had been compounding all week and it felt good to let his mind wander in the fresh air.

Jeremy, out of breath, opened the creaking gate and then ambled over to Kevin's grave first. It was no longer fresh, blending into the lawn perfectly. Trevor's was nearby and all the other boys were in the yard, except one buried in a family plot up in

Nebraska. Jeremy didn't know what to do now that he was there, but it was where he needed to be. He was sure of it.

He sat leaning against the back of a gravestone looking at Kevin's.

"I should have brought you some beer, huh?" he said to the stone and then chuckled. "And a can of Skoal."

Talking to gravestones and the decaying bodies below on prom night. Is this what your life has come to? He shook his head, wishing he had some kind of alcohol. It seemed right. Would a sober person walk two miles to talk to stones and bones? And why would he drink? Would it help him forget what happened by destroying those pesky brain cells that clung onto the horrid details of that night? Or would drinking help to bring him back to those primal emotions? To go back to when the shit hit the fan and relive the moment, but without the filters of the mind that intentionally block negative self-evaluations? Drink up and let the booze dissolve those filters so you can see what a human turd you really are.

Jeremy laughed out loud. These were the deepest thoughts he'd ever had and nobody was around to witness it. Maybe the long walk pushed blood to his usually dormant brain. He laughed some more. It felt good.

He heard thumping in the distance and realized it came from the old gym, location of the prom. He closed his eyes and listened to the far-off music. It was a cycle of mass appeal: country, followed by a pop song, then a classic rock song, and back to country. He hummed to a few of them and for a while stopped thinking. It was pleasant until he imagined his classmates dancing, singing, and having the requisite "time of their lives." Then he thought about Carrie and then the dead boys. Two failures.

Jeremy bundled up in his jacket as the night wore on and beads of dew rose from the ground. He felt he should go home, but after hearing the sounds of tires squealing, he decided to wait. No need to endure the humiliation of being seen walking alone on the road. But the hike ended up not being an option when a police cruiser drove through the graveyard shining its high beam searchlight.

The white light cast long shadows from the gravestones that Jeremy tried to hide in. Then the sheriff heaved himself out of his cruiser and walked through the yard with a foot long MagLight. Moments later he found Jeremy.

"Whatcha doin', son?"

Jeremy looked straight into the beam of light, barely able to discern the outline of the wide man holding it. Blocking the light with his hand he tried to grasp onto words.

"I...uh...just sitting..."

"Sitting and what?"

"What?"

"You're sitting and doing what in this graveyard in the middle of the night?"

"Thinking, sir."

"Stand up, son. Now."

Jeremy did. He had a slight shake. He wasn't sure if it was from the cold or if he was a tad bit frightened. He didn't feel scared, just caught and embarrassed.

The officer shone a light in his eyes.

"How much you been drinking?"

"None at all."

"You expect me to believe that?"

"I'll breathe into a machine...if you want."

"Touch your nose with your right index finger. Slowly."

Jeremy did as he had seen on television.

"Do you want me to do my left, sir?"

"No, you're sober. You mind telling me what you're doing out here? Nobody suppose to be here after sundown. Often have teenagers, usually younger than yourself, come out here and cause trouble."

"No, just thinking."

"I can write you up a citation for trespassing. Just tell me why you're here."

Jeremy looked down at the ground and then towards Kevin's grave. Why was he here?

"I didn't want to stay at home, didn't want to go to the prom either."

"Are you feeling suicidal?"

"What? No. Just started walking and ended up here."

"Did you know the boys that were massacred?"

Jeremy nodded and took a few moments to compose his words. "Worked for a while with Kevin Diamond and his dad. They went to our church and all. I talked to him and that whole group of guys the night they got shot up." Jeremy was surprised he let that out.

"You couldn't have been with them when it happened."

Jeremy felt the blood drain out of his face, but told himself to breathe before answering. He had to be careful. He shook his head.

"Nah, I left before then."

"You didn't come forward?"

"I tried the day after, but I couldn't get inside your office. It was chaotic. And I had nothing to say...nothing that would have helped keep Crazy Eddie behind bars. If anything it would have helped his case. They wanted to hurt him."

The sheriff scratched his chin, thought about it for a moment, and nodded. "You probably did the right thing then. Where do you live? I'll give you a ride home."

Jeremy felt relieved walking to the car. He had finally told law enforcement a little about the massacre, and nothing had happened. Of course the directions would always remain a secret. Always. He plunked down in the passenger seat of the Ford Crown Victoria. It had a musty, masculine smell of sweat and coffee that reminded him of the football coach's office. There was a CB radio on the floor and a shotgun locked to the seats. It felt like a man cave.

"Welcome to my office," Sheriff Dempsey said.

"I like it," Jeremy said.

On the drive they discovered that Jeremy's sister had played softball with the sheriff's youngest daughter.

"Where did your sister go to school?"

"Wichita State. She plays shortstop."

"Good for her. She has a strong arm."

Sheriff Dempsey shook Jeremy's hand before he got out of the car and told him to steer clear of the graveyard at night.

"You're a good kid, Jeremy. Hope to see you again. Now I gotta go find all the drunken troublemakers driving around after prom."

30. A SITUATION

On Monday, Jeremy heard all about the prom. Everybody had a great time, and some went to after-parties that were a blast until they were busted by the police. Classmates asked Jeremy what he did that night.

"I was in bed sick."

"You should have been there, man. You would have felt better," somebody said.

Jeremy nodded, not paying much attention. He had noticed that Carrie looked different when he saw her pass. She had a distant, faraway look. Her shoulders curved inward. She should have been proud with her head held high. As predicted, she and Zack had been named prom king and queen.

Three weeks later, she dropped out of school. With graduation around the corner, it didn't make much sense. Jeremy noticed that Zack was more agitated than usual. When he saw Michelle and asked about Carrie, she looked flustered and said that she was feeling sick. "In a real bad way," she emphasized.

Jeremy emailed Carrie, and then texted a couple of hours later. He told himself it didn't matter what happened to her, it was her own thing. But he felt uneasy, like something bad had happened. He got a text that night at the dinner table. Jeremy immediately jumped up to check his phone on the nearby sofa.

"Isn't there a rule in this house that we don't have phone calls at dinner?" his father said.

Jeremy read the following message: THX 4 MSG. NOT FEELING GR8. THINK I RUINED MY LIFE.

Jeremy felt his heart sink. What did that mean? He typed: DO U WANNA TALK?

Carrie responded: NEED TO BE ALONE NOW. THANK U 4 BEING A FRIEND.

"Jeremy, come to the table and sit down or we'll stop paying for your phone," Gary said.

"Sorry, Dad," Jeremy said going out the door. "This is important."

Jeremy's heart thumped wildly. Was she suicidal? He called again, but she didn't answer. He jumped in his truck and tore off down the road. Carrie was only a few neighborhoods away. He ran a couple of stop signs and saw at least one old man shake a fist at him from his lawn. Pulling up to the curb by Carrie's house, Jeremy decided to call one more time before barging through the door and doing something that might be stupid and embarrassing. He saw Carrie's bedroom light from the second floor window. He dialed, but it went to voicemail after a couple of rings.

"Hey Carrie, it's me. Jeremy. I, uh…well, I'm concerned about you, because the messages you are sending are so…bleak. I want to make sure that everything is okay. That you aren't going to…do anything drastic…to yourself. Not that you would, but if you did, I'd…" Jeremy caught his breath, "I'd be hurt. Big time. It would break my heart because you are…and have always been special to me." Jeremy felt tears welling up in his eyes. "I guess what I'm trying to say is…" he tried to hold it back but couldn't, "that I love you. I always have and always will. Not that I've ever done anything about it. Okay, I'm feel awkward now, but please don't do…"

Jeremy's voice trailed off as he saw Zack Utley's jacked-up truck approaching. Zack was driving with his mother and father in the cab next to him. He hung up when Zack pulled into the driveway, staring daggers at him.

"What's going on?" Jeremy said out loud.

Zack stepped out of his truck and glared at Jeremy. His parents came around to him. They had stern, solemn faces. The front door to the house opened and Carrie's father also displayed a heavy, graven face. Jeremy held Zack's stare. He was not going to blink at that jackass. Something happened at prom. Zack probably got rough with Carrie, trying to get her to give up some nookie, and now Zack is getting a what-for from both parents, Jeremy surmised. Zack's dad grabbed Zack by his arm and jerked him inside. Jeremy hadn't blinked. He had won. The little victory was squashed when he realized a moment later what was really happening.

31. MAN OF HONOR

Jeremy lay in bed all night staring at the ceiling. He felt stung and couldn't shake away the feeling that it was his fault. He believed he had let Carrie down. He should have saved Carrie from Zack and the fate that seemed to hit every twentieth or so Kansas high school girl, according to the news. If he had asked her to the prom, maybe this wouldn't have happened. They'd be in love. And even if it went downhill, she would still go to Kansas State University. But God dealt her an ugly hand, punishing her for being with somebody like Zack.

Jeremy turned over in bed. Why couldn't he do the right thing for once? If he had told Kevin that he didn't know where Crazy Eddie lived, or at least had them drive the opposite direction, things would be different. Same with Carrie: he just needed to ask her to go to the prom and she'd have kept her bright future.

Within a couple of days, news that Carrie and Zack were getting married, shotgun style, was on every high school student's lips. The date was set a few weeks after graduation. People said they were doing it quickly so photos wouldn't show Carrie with too big of a bump. Girls congratulated Carrie on the wedding and talked about dresses, while guys consoled Zack. He had to find a job, in earnest, because there would be three mouths to feed. But from what Jeremy saw, there was a hint of victory behind Zack's woe-is-me act. Neither Jeremy nor Zack mentioned that night at Carrie's when they crossed paths.

"Good luck," was all Jeremy could say.

"Thanks, man. I'm going to need it," Zack said with that jackass smirk.

Zack did better than he should have; Carrie was taking a huge step down.

*

Jeremy found Carrie late one afternoon talking to a gaggle of girls outside the school on a bench. She looked exhausted, while trying to keep a cheery appearance.

"Hey, Carrie."

"Jeremy, how are you doing?" Her eyes seemed to liven.

"Good. I was wondering if I could talk to you alone, in private?"

"You know she's engaged?" Lucy Martin said with snicker.

"There's no ring yet," Jeremy said, and instantly regretted it.

The girls oohed and laughed and then went up a few yards to another bench where they could keep a scandalmongering eye on them.

"So, um, you didn't listen to the message that I sent a while back, did you?"

"I did. It was sweet."

"Well I thought, I don't know. I guess I misinterpreted what your text was about."

"You thought I was suicidal?"

"Kind of."

"Why would I ever do that? How long have you known me?" Her big eyes searched his.

"Most of our lives," Jeremy said. "Well, I didn't know what happened between you and Zack, well, I mean I do know now and…"

Carrie blushed.

"Oh crap, I'm sorry. I'm just digging a deeper hole, aren't I?"

"Maybe a little."

"I guess I just wanted to say, sorry about the message. I didn't mean it. I just overreacted."

"You didn't mean it?" There was a crack in her voice. Her eyes searched Jeremy. He felt panicked. Why did he have to do this? Don't most people just make mistakes and never acknowledge them? Just let that uncomfortableness linger for years and never ever discuss it again? That was the Kansas way, probably the American way, outside of

California and New York and a few other find-your-inner-Buddha states.

"Well no, I mean I meant it. I did, but I..." He heard giggling from the girls not far away and knew his face must have reddened.

Carrie grabbed his hand.

"Hey, it's all right. Under different circumstances, it might have happened: you and me. It just wasn't meant to be. God and His mysterious ways, right?"

Jeremy nodded, telling himself to keep his trap shut.

"Hey, Rogers."

Jeremy turned to see Zack coming their way in long strides. Carrie dropped his hand.

"S'up, Zack. Everything alright?" Jeremy said.

Zack looked back and forth at the two of them. From what Jeremy could tell, Zack's self-esteem would not acknowledge him as a rival, even if he had suspicions. It was over eighty and he was wearing his filthy letterman's jacket. Zack bent down and kissed Carrie on the lips with too much force.

Zack came up for air with a half grin, half snarl. "You two just talkin'?"

"Is that a problem, honey?" Carrie asked. "Jeremy's my oldest friend."

"Just wishing your bride-to-be the best of luck, you know," Jeremy said, staring at Zack's challenging eyes. He wasn't going to blink first this time either.

"And I'm inviting him to be in the wedding as my Man of Honor."

Both Jeremy and Zack whipped around to look at Carrie. She nodded with a huge smile.

"But I, uh…" Jeremy felt sweat trickling down his neck. What was Carrie doing? This was absurd. "I, uh…unfortunately, have a… I regretfully have to decline." He kept his head down. He couldn't look Zack in the eyes now.

"Ah, too bad. I think you'd look good in a dress," Zack said with a snort.

"He wouldn't be in a dress, silly. He'd be in a tux, like your groomsmen."

"What about Michelle? You two have been this close," Zack said, with two fingers together.

"Except those times when we're not," Carrie said, pulling his fingers apart. She turned to Jeremy. "So what do you say? Want to reconsider and be my Man of Honor?"

Jeremy couldn't think of words and knew his face had flushed a deep shade of crimson. The girls from the table were walking over.

"I can't, Carrie. You know I couldn't. Sorry. I gotta get going."

Jeremy tried his best to walk fast without running, but he was sure that he looked like a horse escaping a burning barn.

PART 4

THE LOST YEARS

32. GRADUATIONS

The next week Jeremy wore a red cap and gown, shuffled to the middle of the football stadium with his classmates, and after the speeches (Carrie had resigned as valedictorian to the relief of school officials) crossed the stage when his name was called. He hugged and high-fived friends, colleagues, and everybody around him. He felt weightless, like a heavy anchor had been lifted from his neck. He wouldn't have to retake his senior year and he would own a diploma. Nobody could take that away from him.

Jeremy's family threw a big party with his grandparents, sister, uncles, and cousins crowded in the house. When anybody asked what he planned to do, he'd answer, "mow lawns." That got a big laugh, but he really wasn't looking any further than the summer.

*

Jeremy's sister Jessica graduated the following week from Wichita State with a Bachelor of Education. Her boyfriend, Sam, sat with the family in a stadium where football hadn't been played for more than a decade. He was excessively dressed in a suit and tie, compared to the jeans and T-shirts the family wore in the hot afternoon sun. Ambitious Sam had already become the top junior salesman for John Deere in the South Western Kansas region. He seemed unusually nervous and distracted, saying very little, to Jeremy's relief.

Later, at a long table full of relatives, Sam made an announcement.

"As you all know Jessica and I have been going out for over three years and quite honestly, I could not think of ever going another day without her."

Sam pulled out a small felt box from his pocket. He said a few words about their relationship and time together, but none of that was heard by the family since they were deaf with shock in the noisy restaurant. Jessica, reduced to tears, sobbed and nodded yes. Sam kissed her and put the ring on her finger. Jeremy and the family had expected a proposal at some point soon, but nobody expected it to be made at the Olive Garden.

33. WEDDINGS

A month after graduation, Carrie and Zack were wed. Jeremy attended, sitting with fellow alumni in the Clover United Presbyterian Church. Carrie looked spectacular in the off-white gown and veil. She maintained a brave, plastered smile throughout the ceremony. Zack looked genuinely happy, with a broad smile and puffed-out chest. Afterwards, there was cake and dancing in the assembly hall, but Jeremy excused himself as fast as he could. He didn't want to witness any more than was necessary. He wanted to be alone. He got his wish in spades.

He mowed lawns all summer long, declining any roofing jobs. He moved down to the basement and converted the place into his own man cave. It made perfect sense. Nobody else in the family used it much anymore, and Jeremy spent so much time down there that he often slept on the couch.

Sam and Jessica's engagement, which had been scheduled for mid-October, was moved up to the first week of September. Jeremy, decked out in a tuxedo, served as an usher. Even though he had gained weight, he thought he looked good in formal wear.

Jessica had a few Wichita State softball players as her bridesmaids, while Sam only had his younger brother as his best man. The wedding was held at the Plainview Baptist Church. Dinner and dancing followed at the old gym, where the prom had been held.

A short, stocky girl with bobbed, dyed-red hair and glasses made eyes at Jeremy, and when Jessica had pulled Jeremy reluctantly to the dance floor, he found himself dancing next to her. Although he wasn't initially attracted to her, she was soft and warm when they did a slow dance. He felt electricity running through his body and it was hard to resist her toothy grin.

There was an after-party in somebody's motel room near Emporia, and Jeremy found himself in conversation with the redhead again. Her name was Christie, and she was Jessica's first college roommate.

"What do you do?" she asked him.

"Oh, I, uh, mow lawns, mostly."

"Anything else? After September the grass tends to stop growing."

Her voice was high pitched, but endearing.

"Well, there's a community college in Clover. My parents want me to go, so I'll probably do that. How about you? You've graduated from college, right?"

"I'm not doing anything right now. I have a sociology degree, so employers aren't banging on my door. You know what I mean?"

Jeremy didn't, but he smiled and nodded.

"But I am going to Korea at the beginning of next year," she continued.

"Korea, really? What for?"

"To teach English. It's a two-year program."

"Do you know Korean?"

She shook her head.

"Do you know anybody over there?"

"Nope. But I'm excited. I've never been overseas."

That blew Jeremy's mind. He had rarely been out of Kansas, and never in another country. He was certain he'd never eaten Korean cuisine. Christie didn't even know if she would like it over there, yet she'd signed up for two years. It was crazy. Although she was barely over five feet, she suddenly seemed taller and even more attractive.

Christie invited Jeremy over to her motel room. He felt uncertain walking through the door. It was as nondescript as the room they had left, but now that they were alone with only the dim glow of a bedside lamp, the room seemed like an exotic, foreign bedchamber. She turned to him and he bent down and kissed her. She opened her mouth and pushed her tongue against his mouth. He opened his and tasted the sourness in her tongue. Fiery sensations tingled every inch of his frame and for a brief instant he had an out-of-body experience, realizing that he, Jeremy Rogers, was making out with a woman. They awkwardly kissed and groped for several minutes. He felt the heat radiating from her little body and he sensed she wanted him to do something more, but he wasn't sure what the next moves were.

"Sorry, it's my first time," Jeremy said.

"Oh, really?" she said, and then softened. "It's okay. I don't have too much experience myself."

A moment passed as they stared at each other. Jeremy thought she might throw him out, not wanting to waste her time with the inexperienced.

"I'll start," Christie whispered.

She unbuttoned his shirt. Jeremy felt self-conscious about his stomach pushing over his belt, but she didn't act repulsed as she kissed and rubbed his chest.

She turned her back to him. "Help me out of this."

It was hard to find the tiny zipper in the darkness and even tougher to hold on to it, but he managed to unzip it. She let the straps slide off her shoulders and the dress fell to the floor. She turned to him in her underwear. Jeremy gazed at her curvy body, hoping his jaw wasn't hanging wide open.

"Can you take off my bra?"

Jeremy's throat caught. He nodded instead and told himself he could do it. But he was thrown off when she stepped forward and kissed him instead of turning around. After a moment, she looked up at him.

"What are you waiting for?"

Jeremy fumbled as best he could around her back, trying to figure out the hooks on the strap.

Christie giggled. "Here, I'll do it."

Jeremy felt embarrassed, looking away. He didn't know what he was doing and she could tell. Why hadn't he practiced before? When he looked up and saw Christie's round breasts and touched their warmth, he felt like the luckiest man in the world.

"Let's get you out of these pants," she whispered.

They made clumsy love full of apologies and encouragement. Later, lying in bed with Christie, Jeremy determined that he may have just had the best time of his life. He left her room early in the morning so he could sneak downstairs to his basement bedroom before going to church with his parents. He had a smile all day long.

34. TIME IN A HURRY

Jeremy met Christie for an intense rendezvous in a cheap motel two weeks later. Since she lived in southern Nebraska, they met in Salina, almost in the middle of Kansas. They continued meeting every couple of weeks, when she wasn't working at Starbucks. He had signed up for classes at the community college, but after finding out that attendance was not enforced, he stopped attending by the midterms. He used the classes, however, as an excuse to get out of the house and meet Christie. They had nothing in common, but Jeremy felt lucky for the little bits of time they spent together. Neither of them told Jessica, who was busy with her newly announced pregnancy.

Jeremy was going to be an uncle. It felt weird and too soon, though his mother embraced the idea of being a grandmother. Gary was too stressed out by work to give an honest opinion about it.

At the end of the year, Christie caught a plane from Kansas City to San Francisco International and then on to Seoul. Jeremy had flunked out of KCCC and hardly came up from the basement during the winter. The guilt that both of his parents threw at him for his flunking and joblessness was overwhelming. He emailed Christie almost every day. She told him about her adopted family, the city of Gwangju, new foods she was trying, and so many other new and exciting experiences. Jeremy, unfortunately, rarely had anything interesting to say, and could only reference TV shows or sports. In late February Christie emailed that she had met somebody, but they should still be friends. Jeremy felt more alone than ever.

*

He wasn't sure how it happened so fast, but he was an uncle in early March, mowing lawns in the summer, hibernating in the basement for the winter, and then mowing lawns again. His high school friends who came back from college were about to start their junior year in the fall. He found it hard to talk to Erik and Graham anymore. Not only would they reference history, literature, and current events, but also fraternity parties, roommate situations, and dating women pursuing different degrees. Jeremy got lost in the details of a world he didn't understand. The one person he could talk to was his niece, Kalya. She wasn't even two, but she would watch him intensely when he talked to her and would giggle whenever he acted goofy.

She quickly turned two, then three and four. Talking, walking, and then running. Sam kept advancing at his job, taking on more and more sales territory. He dropped off Kalya to eager grandparents if he was in the area. Jeremy never knew when she was scheduled to come over, but he would be woken by her in the morning, pulling off his bed sheets and wanting to play.

"Unka Jammy, Unka Jammy. Wake up."

Anybody else and he would have been upset, but he couldn't be at his wide-eyed, curly-blond niece.

"Wake up, sleepyhead."

Jeremy would usually pull a blanket over his head and then jump out of bed, chasing Kalya around the basement to her delighted screams. But then Sam was transferred to Omaha, and Jeremy only saw Kalya on holidays. By the time she had turned six, they were out of sync. She didn't dare venture down the basement and he couldn't get her to laugh anymore.

*

When Jeremy turned twenty-five—a quarter of a century old—most of his friends had completed college and were starting families in different towns. Carrie was having her third child. He had seen her at the IGA grocery store, pregnant and carrying a crying baby while the oldest pulled on her other arm, demanding a sugary cereal. She looked haggard and closer to forty, but smiled when he said hello. He felt awkward for her and himself, looking just as disheveled, but without the excuse of children.

Most of the jobs in town were staffed by high schoolers who looked incredibly young. More than one of his customers mentioned that Jeremy should find a new line of work. "Mowing lawns is a kid's job, you know." But where and what?

Then Gary threatened to throw Jeremy out unless he paid rent. He already had to pay his own cell phone bill, which crippled him after the summer. Jeremy couldn't afford rent anywhere, so a compromise was brokered by Gail. Jeremy would do a list of chores each month, from raking leaves to washing their cars or running errands. For every chore not performed, he would have to pay twenty dollars towards rent and board. It was a deal Jeremy grew to hate.

Gary was never satisfied with any work Jeremy did, and he felt like both his parents were constantly yelling at him, telling him to do something every other day. Jeremy wasn't sure when, but at some point his father had lost all of his sensitivity. Jeremy tried to avoid him by surfacing only when he was at work. Gail interceded on Jeremy's behalf every now and then, and even bought the snack foods he loved against Gary's wishes. But she wasn't always an ally, and often she turned on him as well. So when the atmosphere felt too tense, Jeremy stayed in the basement as long as possible, surfacing only to raid the pantry or do the odd job.

Though he already felt outdated and stuck in a cavernous rut, nothing made him feel as old as the day he heard that Crazy Eddie was released from prison.

35. CRAZY EDDIE RETURNS

A chill blasted through Clover when Crazy Eddie was released from prison. It was hard to comprehend that eight years had passed so quickly. The Clover Reporter confirmed the early release. Even though his sentence was for ten years, he was eligible for parole at six, and on the eighth year he was free.

Jeremy received emails from high school friends, including several he had not talked to since graduation. They all wanted to know if Jeremy had any Crazy Eddie sightings. Jeremy reported all the rumors he had heard, even though he rarely ventured outside.

A jacked-up orange Bronco with tinted window had been spotted rolling through Clover. Residents had craned their necks to see if it was Crazy Eddie, but nobody could verify that the "big dude behind the wheel" was he. Also, somebody who knew somebody related to a prison guard said that Crazy Eddie was suspected of killing up to five prisoners, but there were never any witnesses to prosecute him.

A little more than a month after his release, sightings of Crazy Eddie were verified. When he entered the IGA grocery store, parents grabbed their children, pulling them the other direction and telling them to hush. Most people ignored him straightaway, but a few stood ramrod straight and tried to hold a disapproving scowl. Crazy Eddie would stare back with his cold killer eyes until the other person blinked. They always did. By several accounts, it seemed like he was a head taller than anybody else.

Not long after he came back to town, drug use in the next town of Shelby skyrocketed. Then the problem leaked into Clover. It started with a group of twenty-something ne'er-do-wells who began to lose their beer guts and became gaunt and scraggy. Within months, dark circled eyes and yellowish rotten teeth followed, like living zombies—if zombies were jittery. A few of the trailer park crowd where Jeremy had gone to the ill-fated barbeque were labeled as meth-heads. Theft increased, and those caught with the crystals, including two high school football players, would not say where they got it. Nobody had proof Crazy Eddie was the supplier, but it seemed as if he had planned to take down Clover with meth.

The public called on Clover Sheriff Dempsey to do something about Crazy Eddie. However, a recent land survey determined that while the road to the Cooper property resided within the boundary of Clover, the property itself was in Shelby. It was well known that the Shelby sheriff was a corrupt weasel who had a strong hand in his town's politics. It wasn't a surprise that he wasn't in a hurry to investigate Crazy Eddie.

Although Clover residents were upset, it was clear no one was going to confront the huge ex-con. By the end of that summer, every bit of crime and mischief seemed to be attributed to him. Jeremy wouldn't have been surprised if Crazy Eddie would be blamed for the freak snowstorm at the end of September. It seemed like only a matter of time before some big tragic inevitability would happen. It wasn't if, only when.

36. A SIMPLE ERRAND

Jessica and Sam brought Kalya down to Clover for her eighth birthday in late January. Jeremy came up from the basement and watched the Jayhawks battle a close basketball game against the Oklahoma Sooners with Gary and Sam. Gail and Jessica worked in the kitchen on the birthday feast. Kalya probably would have preferred pizza, but fried chicken, buttermilk biscuits, mashed potatoes and gravy, and a chocolate cake were on the menu. The aroma from the kitchen filled the house and made Jeremy's stomach rumble. He couldn't wait to eat, but, like at all family gatherings, he had been asked the same question all day long. Even Kalya asked it. It made him want to stay in bed and eat his stash of Twinkies and Doritos.

"Why don't you have a job, Uncle Jeremy?"

At least Sam had kept his trap shut. Jeremy was certain that he must have a twinge of envy. After all, Jeremy had no mortgage, no children, no nagging wife. But then again, he had no future.

Later, the score was tied at 84 with less than 30 seconds left when the Sooners stole the ball and made a fast break. Then a forward missed an easy slam-dunk, the ball was thrown half court to... Jeremy's mother stepped in front of the television, arms crossed.

"Mom!"

"Gail!" Jeremy's father shouted, craning his neck.

"Jeremy, you had one thing, only one thing to do today."

Jeremy looked around his mother's legs. What was happening?

"Look at me."

He did reluctantly. The game was being interrupted because of him, not her. It wasn't fair.

"What?"

"Don't you remember the one thing you needed to get today?"

Jeremy looked blankly. What the hell could it be? She was always telling him to do something, get something, find something. There were so many somethings that he didn't know which ones to listen to and which ones to ignore.

"Chocolate milk, your only contribution for Kalya's party, for Pete's sake."

"Well, don't sit there," Gary said. "Get up and go get it."

"But the game and—"

"Can I go with Uncle Jeremy?" Kalya said, walking into the room.

"No, Kalya," Jessica shouted from the kitchen.

"But the chocolate milk is for *my* party!"

She stood in front of the television too; her arms were crossed like Gail's.

The crowd went wild on the television. Something big had happened.

"Come on!" Sam shouted.

The rising anger in the room was about to burst.

"Fine," Jeremy said standing. "I'll go."

"Me too!" Kalya said.

There was a collective sigh. The announcer said that viewers had just witnessed a spectacular, once-in-a-decade kind of shot, a shot that nobody in the den had seen. Jeremy felt Sam and Gary scowl.

"Let's go, Kalya," he said, getting out of the room before he was pummeled.

*

Jeremy started up his pickup, letting the heater warm up the interior while he scraped ice off the windshield. Winter had come early and strong, freezing everything since early November. Kalya, already buckled up, had changed the radio station from his heavy metal station to teeny-pop music. She was mouthing the words to an overly produced song by some high-pitched teen idol. He cursed and continued to scrape away.

*

The roads had occasional icy patches, but were manageable. Kalya was a non-stop chatterbox, singing the artificially flavored songs and talking about her first grade class during the instrumental breaks. Jeremy tried to tune out by thinking of all the places he'd rather be. None of them were in Kansas—that was for sure.

"You're fat," Kalya said, bringing Jeremy's attention back to her.

"What?"

"That's what Mom says. She says you don't do anything at all."

"I mow lawns."

"But it's too cold for grass to grow now."

"I rake leaves and shovel snow too."

"When we got to Grandma's house, Mom said you didn't rake the yard."

"She really said that?"

"Yep. She said it looks like Uncle Jeremy is sitting on his big butt again."

Kalya giggled. Jeremy turned down the heat and opened his window. It was getting hot in the cab.

*

He pulled into the IGA grocery store's parking lot, but there was not a single car anywhere. An orange poster board was taped on the window. "Sorry. Pipes broke. Closed due to flooding," with crudely drawn pools of water.

"Does that mean no chocolate milk?" Kalya said with a pout.

"What? No, it means..." He looked at his niece who was almost a foreigner. Even at eight, she was becoming uptight like the rest of the family and no longer the fun and carefree little girl he used to wrestle with. He wanted the old Kalya back. "It means we've got an ice-covered parking lot all to ourselves."

"What's...ayeeeee!"

Kalya squealed as Jeremy hit the gas and braked, sliding several feet. She gripped her seatbelt, eyes wide. He hit the gas again.

"Ayeeeee! No! Stop!"

Jeremy hit the brakes, and they slid. Kalya squeaked.

"Don't do that."

"Nope. No can do," Jeremy said with a devilish grin.

"I'll tell Mom."

"Well you can tell your mom she has a big butt, too!"

Jeremy hit the gas.

"Stop, stop, stop," she said, knuckles white on the seatbelt.

"Not until you put your hands in the air like you just don't care."

"What? Ayeee!"

Jeremy hit the brakes, spinning the wheel of the truck.

"Hands in the air like you just don't care." They spun in a circle.

"I'm scared. Stop it!"

He took his hands off the wheel. "Hands in the air like you just don't care."

"No."

The truck came to a stop, and he accelerated.

"Noooo! Please."

"Hands in the air like you just don't care, say it."

"Hands-in-the-air-don't-care."

"Just don't care," Jeremy corrected.

"Just don't care."

He braked, and they slid.

"Hands up," he said.

"Hands up."

"No, take your hands off the seatbelt."

She shook her head adamantly.

"Come on, hands in the air like you just don't care."

The truck came to a stop. She put her hands up.

"There, are you happy now?"

She stared at him defiantly. So much like her mother.

"Seriously. That's all you're going to do? Not while we're in motion?"

"Yeah."

"Not if I can help it."

Jeremy slammed the gas, racing across the parking lot, and then hit parking brake. The truck spun out of control. Kalya screamed bloody murder. Jeremy saw they were headed for a ditch.

"Hands-in-hair-don't-care!   Hands-don't-care. Just don't…"

He slammed the brakes, turned the wheel back and forth and shifted the Ranger from drive to reverse as they spun circles closer and closer to the ditch. Jeremy closed his eyes as they approached the lip of the deep trench and stopped abruptly on the edge of the grass. Jeremy looked over to Kalya. She still screamed with her eyes shut and hands straight out.

"Kalya, it's okay."

She opened her eyes and looked around, breathing heavily.

"Let's find some chocolate milk."

"No," she said. "Let's do it again."

They smiled at each other, and Jeremy pounded the accelerator.

*

Ten minutes later they drove to the Quick 'N Go not far from the Cooper's property. As Jeremy turned in, an orange Bronco almost clipped the truck as it barreled past in reverse and onto the street before spinning its tires and taking off.

"Is he going sliding on the ice?"

Jeremy watched the Bronco disappear and exhaled. He didn't realize he had been holding his breath.

"No, that was Crazy Eddie Cooper. The meanest, worst man there ever was."

"You pulling my leg?"

"Nope. He was in prison for a few years, but they let him out because he was too crazy inside the jail, beating up everybody. Even the guards were scared of him."

"Really?"

"That's the way I hear it. Listen, let's forget about him and grab some chocolate milk and get back before your big butt mama throws a hissy fit."

*

Inside, Jeremy felt like something was off. The store looked the same. It felt warm, and the fluorescent lights hummed as usual. Jeremy often came here for a Dr. Pepper or a fill up. He had even considered asking about the "Help Wanted" sign that hung in the window, but he knew he wouldn't make it a week into the job—counting money, cleaning up messes, restocking cups and lids—he couldn't do it. There was too much responsibility, and so many things he'd screw up.

"Look, Uncle Jeremy, there's the chocolate milk."

Kalya ran to the refrigerated section while Jeremy tried to figure out what was bugging him. He walked to the counter to find the cash register open and empty. And Shirley Simplot, sixty-something, who always asked about his parents, lay on the ground with her head bleeding.

"Uncle Jeremy, which one should I get? Uncle Jeremy?"

He walked behind the counter. Bending over he touched her neck, trying to find a pulse.

"Shirley. Hey."

She blinked and touched her head. She seemed dazed as she stared at her bloody fingers.

"Are you okay, Shirley?"

"I'm not sure."

"I'll call an ambulance."

Jeremy dialed 911 when Kalya started babbling again.

"Uncle Jeremy, Uncle Jeremy!"

"Just get whichever one you want. I don't care… Yes. An emergency. At the Quick 'N Go at—"

"Uncle Jeremy, Uncle Jeremy, the crazy guy is coming back!"

"What?"

Jeremy followed his niece's gaze to the window. The orange Bronco was racing toward the store.

"Kalya, get away from the window now!" Jeremy dropped the phone and grabbed Shirley.

"Can you stand?"

Shirley nodded, and Jeremy hefted her to her feet just as the Bronco jumped the curb and crashed into the store. Glass and junk food flew everywhere. Kalya screamed.

"Kalya, where are you?"

She ran to them behind the counter and turned ghost white upon seeing Shirley. Then they all turned to the Bronco with its nose in the store and shards of glass all around it. They looked at Crazy Eddie behind the wheel, and he looked at them. Crazy Eddie looked much older and his gaunt face was covered with a full beard and a couple of blue teardrop tattoos under each intense tiny pupil. They all held the stare for several seconds. Jeremy heard the faint voice of the dispatcher over the phone asking if everything was okay. Then Crazy Eddie turned and brought up a shotgun. Jeremy grabbed Kalya's hand and supported Shirley as they headed for the "Employees Only" door.

Shutting the door, Jeremy saw the muscular 6'9" frame of Eddie Cooper bounding into the store with his shotgun in hand.

"Where's the key to lock the door? Where is it?" Jeremy shouted.

"Here," Shirley said, pulling a key on a lanyard attached to her belt. He grabbed it, pulling her to the door. As soon as Jeremy locked it, the doorknob turned and then several kicks followed.

"We're going to have to reinforce—" he said as a shotgun blast punched a hole in the middle of the door. Splinters of wood somersaulted in the air, most of them missing Jeremy by inches. Kalya squealed.

"Is there a back door?"

Shirley pointed to a wall with stacks of boxed soda pop concentrate.

"There, but I don't have a key to that door. Greg's never given it to me."

Crazy Eddie slammed his body against the employee's door. Jeremy's mind raced. He looked around the small storage area stacked full of plastic wrapped snacks, boxes of concentrate for the fountain machine, and beverages on cardboard trays. There was a steel door to his left with a note stating rules about refrigerator safety. Jeremy didn't want to freeze to death hiding in there if he could help it.

"Let's barricade this door," Jeremy said, nodding his head at the shot punctured door, "and hope it holds until the police come."

He hauled the soda concentrate against the door along with trays of canned soda pop and beer, while staying low to avoid shotgun blasts that caused fountains of sticky syrup to cascade on the floor. The door held.

Kalya shivered in the far corner of the room. "Why's he doing this?"

"It's…complicated, Kalya," Jeremy said, trying to keep his voice steady and calm. "He's always been mean."

"Awful quiet now," Shirley said, holding a bloodied rag to her head. "Do you suppose he left?"

"Dunno, but I'm not opening this door until the police get here."

Jeremy found a wet mop and worked to remove blobs of the syrup covering his jeans. Then they heard sounds coming from the walk-in refrigerator. Jeremy and Shirley looked at each other.

"You think he's just stealing some beer?"

Jeremy shook his head. He took hold of the stainless steel handle of the refrigerator door and opened it. He saw Crazy Eddie trying to force his colossal body through the shelves of milk. He shoved gallons and cartons of milk to the floor with his shotgun. Jeremy looked into his pinhole pupils.

"I'm going to get you, Jeremy Rogers. Can't have no witnesses. Ain't going back to prison again."

Jeremy slammed the refrigerator door shut. No witnesses? What was he talking about?

"We need to get out of here."

He pulled the gooey boxes away from the "Employees Only" door, piling them against the refrigerator door. Jeremy pulled, heaved, and shoved, feeling like that Greek guy who kept doing the same thing over and over again. Who was that guy? Socrates? Napoleon? He got the ladies through the blasted door and puddles of goop as Eddie began slamming against the refrigerator door.

The barricade held long enough for them to get to the truck. Jeremy shook so much it took three tries before he got the key in the ignition. Crazy Eddie staggered out with a shotgun in one hand and chocolate milk in the other, the brown liquid trailing down his bearded chin.

"It's on, Rogers! Oh it's on," he shouted.

He aimed the shotgun, but Jeremy threw the truck in reverse and flew away from the gas station and into the road, not unlike that orange Bronco five minutes earlier. Crazy Eddie blasted the shotgun wide of the truck and howled like a wolf.

37. WHAT MATTERS

Jeremy sped along the icy streets towards town.

"Where we going, Uncle Jeremy?"

"To the police before we get Shirley to the hospital. If that's all right with you, Shirley?"

"Don't worry about me. Let's get that monster in jail first."

But they never made it into town. Barreling through a stop sign, Jeremy saw the orange Bronco expanding in his rearview mirror. "Crap!"

"What?" Kalya asked.

Jeremy floored the gas, but his pickup's four cylinders were no match for a V-8. The Bronco slammed into the back of the pickup, causing it to swerve.

Kalya screamed.

Careening around a curve, the Bronco clipped the side bumper, causing the Ranger's rear wheels to lose traction and spin.

"Hands-in-the-air-like-you-just-don't-care!" Kalya shouted involuntarily as the truck hurtled out of control, spinning in tight circles and taking out a barbed wire fence. When the truck stilled, they found themselves in the middle of a frozen pond. The tires whirled in vain, unable to purchase a grip. Jeremy tried reverse, stomping on the gas pedal and then easing on it. Nothing. Jeremy locked eyes with Shirley. Is this how it ends? Kalya, who had been hyperventilating, caught her breath and let out a piercing scream.

"Calm down, Kalya. Okay, listen. We've gotta get out of this truck."

"This ice can't be solid," Shirley said.

"What does that mean?" Kalya asked, wide-eyed.

"Maybe the pond isn't deep," Jeremy said. "I mean, the ice is holding the truck, isn't it?"

The unmistakable crack of breaking ice caused tears to streak down Kalya's cheeks.

"Everybody out," Jeremy said.

Twenty yards away, Crazy Eddie pulled up to the edge of the ice. Jeremy didn't know what to do, but he knew he had to protect Kalya. It was the thing that mattered most.

Jeremy turned to Shirley. "I know I didn't ask this earlier, and it's quite obvious, but you don't happen to have a cell phone...or a gun?"

"Left both of them at the store," Shirley said. "Getting hit in the head don't make you right when you need to be."

"At least you've got an excuse."

They shared a quick smile. Jeremy had lost his cell over a year ago from unpaid bills.

"Shirley, you take Kalya to the other side over there."

"What you are going to do?"

Jeremy pulled out a tire iron from under the seat. It felt heavier than it ever had. "Try to negotiate with a mass murdering meth head. Just go."

Shirley and Kalya gingerly stepped out of the truck and onto the ice.

"Be careful, Uncle Jeremy."

"You too, Kalya."

Jeremy stood on the slick surface on the pond. Cracks surrounded all the tires, but no water seeped through. Not yet.

Across the bank, Crazy Eddie was climbing over to the passenger side of the Bronco since his driver's side door was blocked by a tree. Jeremy glanced back and saw Kalya and Shirley cautiously shuffling toward the shore. *Get across to the other side*, he wanted to shout. *Just get across*. He had to make sure they made it across. Then it hit him. This is it. This is what it is all about. His waste of a life finally had purpose. The endless hours of video games and reality TV schlock, not asking Carrie to the prom, flunking community college, and all of the other missed opportunities to live life and be somebody. He gripped the tire iron. It would lose to a shotgun anytime, but…he had to do something.

"Hurry up!" he finally shouted to his niece and Shirley.

When he turned, Crazy Eddie was on the ice, walking towards him. Jeremy inhaled a deep, cold breath and took a step forward, ready for fate to deal its hand, when Crazy Eddie slipped. He dropped the shotgun and in a thunderous boom it discharged sideways on the ice, sending the shot and lead pebbles skipping across the pond. This is the time, Jeremy thought. The pump action lay on the ice. With the pipe, he might have an advantage. Maybe, if he could land a precise swing on top of his head. A complete knock out. If not, then…well, Crazy Eddie would grab the tire iron and beat him into hamburger meat.

Crazy Eddie stood, dusting the ice off of his jeans. He looked at Jeremy before reaching into his pocket and pulling out a plastic baggie. He fished out crushed white crystals and snorted.

"Want some?" he asked, as if offering a piece of gum.

"Uh, no thanks, Eddie."

He put the baggie away and shook himself. "You know. It's not that I want to do this, but I gotta. I can't have any witnesses. I ain't going back to jail again."

"Eddie, you'll be going back to jail anyway. If you kill us, it'll be a murder charge, not just robbery, assault, and battery."

"But you're the witnesses."

Jeremy wanted to laugh at the meth logic, but he had to try to reason with him. "There's a video of you back at the store, plus your fingerprints have to be all over the place."

Eddie looked perplexed. "How do you know so much?"

"I watch TV. A lot of TV."

Crazy Eddie looked up at the sky as if counting clouds and then reached into his pocket for the baggie. He took another snort and picked up the shotgun. Jeremy felt his grip on the tire iron weaken. Holy crap. Shirley and Kalya were on the shore. Mission accomplished, right? Jeremy started to back away from his truck. He noticed water seeping through the cracks of the ice. It wasn't frozen solid.

"I gotta do this, Rogers. Nothing personal," He said taking a cautious step towards Jeremy. "You were always nice to me. Better than most. You and Carrie and…that faggy kid were the only friends I had over. Maybe the only friends I ever had in school."

Jeremy felt touched for a momentary second, but realized he needed to stall or run for it. He couldn't dodge a shotgun blast, but the further he got, the less the pellets would penetrate.

Crazy Eddie started to walk towards him.

"Hey Eddie, uh, friends don't shoot friends you know."

"It ain't like that, Rogers. I got a parole officer and if he finds out—"

"He's gonna find out, Eddie. There's a difference between robbery-assault and murder. I'm talking about you frying in the electric chair."

"A stainless-steel ride."

"What?" At least Crazy had stopped, the barrel pointed down at a forty-five-degree angle.

"Lethal injection. That's what them on death row call it."

Crazy Eddie gave him a look like he was stupid. Jeremy shrugged. He learned something new. But he needed to keep this going.

"Any other words in prison you learned?"

The ex-con belted out a huge laugh. "It's a new language in there. Take me all day to teach you. But you're stallin', Rogers, and I got to finish business."

He raised the shotgun and took a step forward. With a crash, the front end of the Ranger broke through the ice behind Jeremy. He heard Kalya's scream in the distance. Water seeped through additional cracks that rapidly splintered from the center of the pond. Jeremy slid to his stomach, trying to distribute his weight. Crazy Eddie stopped for a moment, and then kept walking. Jeremy estimated he had to be over 250 pounds. He gripped the tire iron. One swing. Maybe two.

When Crazy Eddie was two feet away, he leveled the shotgun. Jeremy waited.

"Sorry, man. It's business," Crazy Eddie said as he pulled the trigger.

Click.

Jeremy raised up and swung the iron across Crazy Eddie's hand before he could pump a shell into the chamber. Crazy Eddie dropped the gun and howled, staring at his broken fingers. Jeremy swung again, smashing the giant's knee. The iron popped out of Jeremy's hand and slid on the ice. Crazy Eddie hobbled, screaming curses, and grabbed on to the unsubmerged back end of the truck.

"You're a dead man, Rogers. Dead."

Jeremy looked at the shotgun and the tire iron. Both were several feet away. He crawled to the shotgun and pumped a shell into the chamber.

He turned and pointed the gun at Crazy Eddie.

"Come on, Rogers. It ain't in you," he said. "You don't fool me."

The ice gave way. Crazy Eddie and the entire truck fell through. Jeremy scrambled on his belly across the freezing wet ice towards the shore. Looking back, Crazy Eddie shouted and howled, trying to grip the edge of the ice as the truck sank.

Sheriff Dempsey and a deputy pulled up seconds later. They threw a rope to the drowning man from the shore. He held onto it as he was dragged out of the hole and across the ice. He was shaking so bad from hypothermia that he was no longer a threat, though handcuffs were applied before he was put in the ambulance. Through chattering teeth, he kept repeating, "Can't have no witnesses."

Shirley was also taken to the hospital after a bandage was applied by the EMTs.

The sheriff looked out at the pond and the large hole with just an inch of the Ranger's cab cresting.

"We'll tow the truck out for you, but I'm sure it's nothing but scrap now." He turned to look at the orange Bronco. "We'll be confiscating that Bronco, and after is all said and done we might work out an arrangement where you could be driving it."

Jeremy nodded. It would be an upgrade.

"I'm also going to need an official statement. It can wait until the morning if you don't mind coming in."

"Sure."

"You showed a lot of courage today," the sheriff said, looking at him. "What do you do for a living?"

Jeremy swallowed. It seemed like this question would dog him the rest of his life. "Unemployed for the moment. I work mostly in the summer."

The sheriff nodded, taking it in. "Have you ever considered wearing a uniform to work?"

Jeremy was confused. What was the sheriff talking about?

"A job in law enforcement?"

This took Jeremy by surprise. He hadn't, at least not since he was five.

"No, sir, I haven't."

"You might consider it. We can talk about it tomorrow."

38. HERO

During dinner, a few hours later than scheduled, Kalya talked nonstop about the adventure she'd had. She painted her uncle as brave and unwavering. For the first time, Jeremy sensed respect from his father, mother, sister, and even Sam. It felt strange and awkward. It was too new to comprehend, like waking up with a third arm.

"Well, there is one thing that didn't happen today—we still don't have any chocolate milk," Sam said, which caused an uproar of laughter at the table.

"It's okay," Kalya said. "It wasn't that important."

*

Calls came in before the birthday cake was cut from people in Clover and the media around the state. Jeremy was being hailed as a hero. He fielded calls for over two hours, repeating the line that he was just trying to protect his family and friends.

"It wasn't a big deal. Anybody else would have done the same thing."

By the third interview, Jeremy was on autopilot, but his mind was on what Sheriff Dempsey had said. Was there really a possibility he might get a job as a deputy? What were the qualifications? He tried to picture himself in the brown Clover uniform, but couldn't.

Later that night, when Jeremy went down to the basement and looked at his room, he was disgusted. How did he live in such squalor? Clothes were heaped in piles, with snack wrappers and empty soda-pop bottles littered everywhere. He wanted to sleep somewhere else, not on the bed with sheets that hadn't been changed in several months. He couldn't be the person he had been earlier that morning. He needed to change, whether he was offered a deputy position or not.

In the morning, after he showered, Jeremy borrowed his father's razor so he could get a closer shave than usual. He wished he had a haircut as he did his best to part it and keep it down. He wished he had done a lot of things differently, so many things.

He put on his least wrinkled dress shirt and a tie, and then walked upstairs.

"Do you want breakfast before you go?" Gail asked as he grabbed the doorknob, about to step outside.

"What? Sorry, I didn't hear you." Jeremy looked out the window at the media vans that had parked outside of the house.

"Would you like some breakfast?"

"I'd better not. My stomach is too jumpy."

"Did you see that you're a local hero?" Gary said, holding up the Kansas City Star. He had a smile on his face, which Jeremy hadn't seen directed at him in years. "Take a look."

Jeremy took the paper and looked at the article. It read: "Clover Man Saves 2 From Massacre Felon." His senior high school picture was printed next to Crazy Eddie's prison photo. He stared at his eighteen-year-old self—the one who got it all wrong.

"You look nice. Like you're going for a job interview," Gail said.

Jeremy set the paper down, but he couldn't take his eye off of his picture.

"Yeah, who knows? Maybe I am."

THE END

ACKNOWLEDGMENTS

I would to thank several people who helped make this book happen.

First and foremost is Jay Hartman of Untreed Reads. He rejected my short story "Eggnog" for the anthology *The Killer Wore Cranberry*, but then asked me to expand on the story and make it into a novella. *Lost in Clover* wouldn't exist without him.

Thank you to Pat Morin for letting me know about Untreed Reads. I'd also like to thank the first readers of my rough draft: Alex, Amulet, Andy, Dylan, Kevin, and Sachin. And a big thanks to Stephen and Sarah, whose critiques firmed up the final draft.

Finally, a huge shout out to Teresa, who deals with my misuse of commas, missing articles, and personal infractions…yet still sticks around. Lucky me.

Made in the USA
Las Vegas, NV
01 February 2022

42798138R00115